# FABULOUS LIVES STORIES

First published in Australia in 2019
by Margaret River Press
PO Box 47
Witchcliffe WA 6286

www.margaretriverpress.com
email: info@margaretriverpress.com

Copyright © Bindy Pritchard

The moral right of the author has been asserted.
This book is copyright. Apart from any fair dealing for the purpose of private study, research, criticism or review, as permitted under the Copyright Act, no part may be reproduced by any process without written permission. Enquiries should be made to the publisher.

Cover design by Debra Billson
Edited by Josephine Taylor
Printed in Australia by McPherson's Printing Group
Published by Margaret River Press

Cataloguing-in-Publication entry data is available from the
National Library of Australia

A catalogue record for this book is available from the National Library of Australia

trove.nla.gov.au

This publication has been made possible with funding from the Department of Local Government Sports and Cultural Industries

Department of
**Local Government, Sport
and Cultural Industries**

ISBN: 978-0-6484850-4-9

Bindy Pritchard is a Perth-based writer whose short fiction has appeared in various anthologies and literary journals such as *Westerly*, *Kill Your Darlings* and *Review of Australian Fiction*. Her stories have been shortlisted in numerous writing competitions, and she was runner-up in both the Margaret River Short Story Competition and *HQ Magazine/* Dymocks Short Story Award. Bindy has a Graduate Diploma in Creative Writing from Curtin University.

*for Sandy*

# BINDY PRITCHARD
# FABULOUS LIVES STORIES

MARGARET RIVER
·PRESS·

# CONTENTS

| | |
|---|---|
| **THE SHAPE OF THINGS** | 1 |
| **DYING** | 20 |
| **HAPPY DAYS** | 29 |
| **FABULOUS LIVES** | 48 |
| **BEES OF PARIS** | 66 |
| **IN TRANSIT** | 79 |
| **THE EGG** | 91 |
| **THE RETURNING** | 104 |
| **MONKEY PUPPET** | 122 |
| **ARROW** | 136 |
| **IN MEMORIAM** | 148 |
| **GODDESS OF FIRE AND WIND** | 169 |
| **WARM BODIES** | 182 |
| **SEA WRACK** | 204 |
| **THREAD** | 217 |
| **LAST DAYS IN DARWIN** | 225 |
| **ACKNOWLEDGEMENTS** | 237 |

# THE SHAPE OF THINGS

When Leonie found the young man lying outside her ground floor apartment he was naked and perfect, and when she felt his pulse for a sign of life there was still a warmth in his skin that made her wonder if he was alive, or was it the residual afternoon sun in the concrete that was reheating him like leftovers? It was too early for foot traffic; city workers were still caught up in meetings or texting friends from bus shelters. With no expert to defer to, no alpha male to take on the responsibility, Leonie knew everything now rested with her. She knelt over the body, spanned her hands like butterfly wings across his sternum, found the heart, and began to pump. Thirty beats and two breaths, or was it fifteen beats to two breaths? She settled for twenty, starting slowly and then increasing the pace to match the rhythm of the Bee Gees song 'Stayin' Alive', something an instructor at a workplace first aid training course had taught her years ago. She could still think of other things though; it was uncanny how the mind worked in that way, thoughts still twisting through the action of CPR. She thought of the gays on the third floor, the girl who left a copy of *Water for Elephants* at the laundromat, and whether there was a reporter from *Today Tonight* hiding behind the Moreton Bay fig ready to expose her on national TV because she was supposed to be on sick leave. Two minutes passed by, and nothing happened. She pumped his beautiful hairless chest, a perfect male torso triangle, and willed whatever life-force she could gift from her hands into this younger body. A pity for him to die now, she thought.

'What happened?'

Leonie didn't stop, managed to still keep up with the Bee Gees as she glanced at the guy leaning over her. She recognised him as one of the men from the third floor—*Gavin*, he'd told her one day, unasked.

'I think he fell,' she answered.

'Do you know him?'

'No. I thought he was one of your lot.'

'If only.'

It didn't seem right for him to talk in this way. She wished she had a blanket to cover the young man's nakedness.

'Is he dead?' Gavin bent over the body and Leonie could see the failed plugs dotting his sweaty bald head.

'Not sure.'

'I can see his muscles twitching. Is that normal?'

'The muscles have memory,' she said, though she wasn't sure if she'd read that in connection with exercise.

'Must be a good memory.'

It was something in his voice, a sardonic, lewd knowingness that made Leonie stop pumping and look down between the man's legs to where his penis grew erect like a giant pink cobra. She stared at the wonder of science, how the blood must pour into all the extremities of the body in a last-ditch attempt at procreation, the way it did after she got sick, and on the day before her operation when she'd bled through a packet of Libra. But then she heard the groan, saw the fair eyelashes flicker away the sunlight, and knew that he was slowly traversing back into consciousness.

'He's alive!' Gavin moved closer, breathing oily pleasure over them. In the sunshine, his textbook moustache had the flat colour of a home dye job. Leonie could almost feel his greasy pores gape and wink at the young man.

'Can you get him a blanket and some water?' she asked, making her voice strong and masculine.

'Sure thing.'

'I'll call an ambulance,' she yelled out, watching him lope away, his body not a triangle but a hulking, overworked frame.

She never got to call the ambulance. The young man sat up, shook his head as if to shed some unwanted memory, and stared at his erection like it was a strange creature.

'Are you okay?' she asked, searching him for any visible signs of trauma.

'I must have fallen.'

'From the third floor?'

'No. Not the third,' he said, and she felt the relief flood her chest.

'Do you live around here?'

'No.'

'What's your name?'

'I can't say.'

Leonie wasn't used to such mysteries in life. Her own was there for all to see. Toothy gaps in a picket fence, an iron gate opening into a small front courtyard with a bike, and a single director's chair that used to be red but had now faded to salmon pink, where lately she sat each morning dressed in her jammies drinking a cup of chamomile tea and watching the workers hurry by. There was nothing sinister in her leading him through the open gate, nor telling Gavin—when he came calling by much later with a fluffy pillow, bottle of Mount Franklin and the smell of the shower fresh on his skin—that the young man was fine and being watched over by family members.

If you walked by later that evening, it should have been possible to see a woman's head bobbing at the kitchen sink window, but tonight the curtains in the living room were firmly drawn—over-drawn, so that not even the glow of the television could escape the double-banked edge of fabric.

\* \* \*

The young man had nowhere to go. It was as simple as that, thought Leonie, as she mashed the avocado into the light sour cream and added the chopped tomato and taco seasoning. He gave no name, no hint of an address, told her nothing of his circumstances. She wondered if he was running away from family or hiding from a drug dispute, a mugging, but somehow she doubted that. He didn't have the look of the hunted or haunted. Like a small child, he had allowed her to lead him by the arm into her place, into a chair in front of the television with that unquestioning, open look that suggested he was willing to take in anything proposed. Like his nakedness for instance. He took that in his stride—and the offer of a T-shirt and trackie pants. She carried the dip to him, slightly conscious of the fact she was making an effort, going through the motions of entertaining, something which she hadn't done for some time—not since the operation, when a couple of work colleagues had paid her a polite perfunctory visit. Even then she never offered any food, wanting them to quickly leave her small apartment, which was infected with the sour odour of her illness.

'I think you should stay tonight,' she suggested.

'Okay.'

He took little nibbles of food, eating gingerly and being careful not to make crumbs on the furniture. God, he's barely a man, she observed, imagining the kind of childhood training his mother must have recently imparted. Seventeen?

Nineteen? It was hard to tell his age; his face was soft like a boy's but his body belied its manhood.

'You can stay longer if you like.'

'Sure.' He stared unblinkingly at Leonie, drinking her in with his pale blue eyes until she felt he had seen enough. She wasn't used to being looked at in such a strong single dose.

She went to busy herself in the kitchen and catch her breath. Those eyes. They were of an exquisite paleness, a paleness she normally associated with people without depth, a certain stupidity—'the lights are on but no-one's home' kind of blue. Had he lost his memory? She knew she would spend half the night restless and awake, checking all the internet news sites. Anyone who had eyes like that, who looked as amazing as that, would surely be missed. All those Facebook and Twitter accounts would be firing across one billion optic fibres tonight.

\* \* \*

In the days leading up to Mardi Gras there was always a feverish energy in the air, like the countdown before a prom or a wedding, when people with a future got pleasure from making plans. You could feel it at cafés; hear it on trains, in hotel lobbies, from men dressed in tailored suits—the air was thick with it. It was hard to move through the gossipy streets. Not even the shrill blanket blue of the sky could take the edge off that sticky expectancy. Was it always this potent, wondered Leonie as she hurried to buy some supplies: some fresh labne at the local deli, a rack of lamb to marinate with sprigs of rosemary and garlic—having a bit of a splurge, as her mother would say. Thirty years ago it had felt different. Less crowds, and a free viewing of the small number of gay and lesbian pride floats. Nowadays, a trendy and straight crowd paid a premium for the right to sit at upmarket bars and restaurants on Oxford Street to watch the spectacle unfold as if it was merely street performance.

Leonie went into her favourite deli, averting her eyes from the swinging mirrored doors as always, and saying hello to the same woman standing behind the counter, whose name she still didn't know after all these years. The woman wore a hijab, a brightly patterned swathe of cloth, and without hair or the sense of a skull her face seemed like a framed snapshot of a vulnerable, much younger self. She was always polite to Leonie. Each week they shared the same sort of conversation about weather and weekends as if they both were rehearsing a cultural expectation, and in the background Leonie had the feeling that a husband or father listened in. She examined the cuts of meat, the slabs that had been drained halal style and smelled cleaner, fresher than at the larger supermarkets. There were tubs of glossy olives, pyramids of fried, cigar-shaped pastries, ceramic bowls of hummus, and salads sun-drenched in colour, and when Leonie asked for a serve of tabouli for two, the woman didn't blink but overstuffed it into the medium-sized takeaway container so that it squeaked under the plastic lid.

The shopping bags were heavier than usual, and as the surgeon had warned her not to carry more than five kilos Leonie stopped along the way home, sitting at benches or on café chairs and releasing the plastic bags from her arms, where the loops had cut ugly red indentations into the skin. She realised she was now sitting opposite the laundromat, the place where she came to wash heavier items like her sheets and towels ever since her old Whirlpool had seized up, and where she was forced to wait for the whole wash and dry cycle. It was too risky to leave, she'd found, because sometimes stuff would go missing or, worse, loads would be removed halfway through a cycle and dumped onto the floor.

Leonie noticed that someone had pasted copies of the same poster over the windows, so that it looked like a series of postage stamps: a hot-pink triangle in a green circle, captioned 'This is a homophobic free zone'. She wondered if it was the girl she saw last week, the one covered in an armoury of piercings who tipped out her dirty clothes from a khaki surplus bag, so that a musky taint invaded the room. She asked Leonie for change—they always did—and Leonie had begrudgingly given her two one-dollar coins. The girl was no different to those itinerants who drifted in and out each fortnight: English backpackers dressed in midriff tops with tans verging on sunburn, or local druggies pale skinned and all in black. But what made this girl stand out was the novel she was reading. *Water for Elephants*. She sat and read the whole time, never taking her eyes away from the pages, only stopping to transfer the washing across to the dryer. When it was time to leave, the girl left the book on the cracked plastic chair and Leonie didn't know whether she had forgotten it, or had deliberately discarded it, discovering that there was nothing in the lightweight pages for her after all.

When Leonie finally made it back to the apartment with her groceries, Gavin and another man were circling the pavement in her small courtyard. They didn't have the decency to look surprised.

'Any news about the boy?'

She frowned at the men. Gavin's friend was a smaller compact version of him: the same overworked body, the same simian gait.

'I haven't heard a thing.'

Gavin shot a knowing look at his friend. 'Are you sure? A little birdie told us otherwise.'

'I have no idea what you're talking about.' Leonie's voice rose with the indignation of someone who is clearly lying.

'Tell the beautiful boy we're having a party tonight.'

That she didn't doubt. There were parties most nights on the third floor. She quickly unlocked the door, and banged it shut behind her. She hesitated, sensing the men still there on the other side. Inside the apartment it was deathly quiet. Too quiet, and she panicked about not taking the young man to the hospital straightaway for a brain scan, but there he was, still asleep on the sofa, his soft breath leaving a light film on the television screen. Or pretending to be asleep, for she could see the curtains had been moved slightly apart so that a narrow shaft of light now entered the room. Leonie went to the kitchen, flicked the switch and then pulled down the stiff blind, the sensation of grease and dust tingling at her fingers.

'What are you doing?'

He had startled her, coming up behind without a sound. He looked sleepy and tousled and she felt a tug of desire as she remembered his erection.

'Look, is there someone I should ring? Let them know you're all right?'

'Is it still okay to stay?'

'Yes. Yes. Of course.' She hurried the words out, knowing that things would get tight in two weeks when the sick leave ran out. 'Do you have a headache?' she remembered to ask. 'You have to tell me if you notice any onset of sudden pain.'

'It's sore here,' he said, lifting up his shirt and pointing to the two bruised shadows beneath his shoulder blades.

'You must have fallen on your back. You don't remember anything?'

'I don't remember,' he said, and from the clarity in his eyes she thought he was telling the truth.

'I can fix your pain.' Leonie fetched her toiletries bag (she hadn't bothered unpacking since the hospital), and brought out the cornucopia of meds: tramadol, naproxen, analgesics and the pièce de résistance—oxycodone, poor man's heroin. 'What's your drug of choice?'

'Are *you* in pain?'

The question caught her by surprise. 'Always.'

The truth was that the pain was no longer an issue. The removal of her entire womb had seen to that. But Leonie still saw herself in terms of her illness. Endometriosis. The years of bracing herself for the agony every month, the rogue bits of wandering uterine lining, which stuck to unlikely places—her bowels, her lungs, her brain—starting little bleeds in a futile attempt to replicate life.

She handed the young man two analgesics, for a lower-grade pain, and he took them dutifully, like a good boy. What to do with him, she thought. With this blank canvas, this enigma who gave nothing of himself away, she knew she would be the one to carry the conversation tonight, and that would be exhausting.

\* \* \*

Where to begin? It was always easiest to start with your job, so Leonie began telling him about her work at the government department. Coordinator of Youth Programs, the same job for twenty-five years, though over the years there had been some changes: different job titles, job descriptions, and the altered spelling of the word 'program' to 'programme' whenever a Liberal government came into power. There was another worker who shared the same small office space, who sat back to back with Leonie, and there was always this false sense that they were connected by more than the static in their hair and the bulk of their ergonomic chairs. For the past two years it was Joan, and before that Vivian, with the tins of no-drain tuna 'tasters', and then Shelley, young and breezy, who had laughed at the word 'petticoat'. The clients, too, had changed, yet stayed the same. Disenfranchised, disaffected, damaged teenagers needing ten good reasons to stay in work or school. Money was thrown at their department, then subsequently cut, and it was exhausting year in, year out, trying to manage the ebb and flow of their fortunes. The stress took its toll. Leonie found it hard to switch off at night, took the heavy files home for bedtime reading, contacted client families on weekends. Got too involved.

'So you hate your job?' he asked her, and Leonie replied rather defensively, 'No. No.'

Not exactly hate, but the frustration of knowing there was no place she'd been that had made a difference; the feeling of pushing dirt around, into different corners of a room.

She also felt like a fraud. It would have been better to have had a background in social work or youth counselling, but instead she came in on a generic public service examination and her university major, Gender Studies.

'What's that?' he asked, and she couldn't help but laugh.

'You know, how we construct ideas about the masculine and the feminine.'

He stared, looking confused.

'Kristeva, Irigaray and Cixous?' Leonie picked the names out of the air like exotic fruit.

'Tell me,' he asked, so she started to explain about the university she attended in the eighties, the new institution that was supposed to break with academic tradition. Not just in its architecture (the prefabricated buildings, a scraggly bush court), but reflected in the course names, like 'Semiotics of Art', and 'Body, Place and Post-Colonial Experience'. The year was 1984, and it was the first time she had heard about the Politics of Desire, Lacanian theory or 'semiotic', a word that reminded her of 'amniotic': a salty, safe fluid to float in. These studies were like a gift to her—what else could help a girl who was as plain and ordinary as a moth?—and when she hacked off her Catholic-school plaits and grew out the dark stubble on her legs she knew it was more about this feeling of belonging than shocking her poor conservative mother in the suburbs.

There were more women than men in the course and they met at lunchtime in the refectory, a diverse group of school-leavers and mature-aged students—some newly divorced, others clearly in love—where they would sit and drink coffee and discuss ideas. She remembered a black-painted feature wall where each semester slogans were added and rubbed over in chalky hieroglyphs. Once it was the female Venus symbol, and then a large pink triangle, a reminder of what Hitler had done to the homosexuals in concentration camps, making them wear a portion of the Jewish Star of David to mark (or was it mock?) their sexual orientation. The symbols sparked something inside them all, emboldened them to take their protests off the campus, to the car parks outside abortion clinics and then onto the streets of Sydney, where their cries morphed into anthems of celebration.

At her first Mardi Gras, Leonie followed the others down a rainbow-painted path, like Dorothy on the road to discovery, and there she saw floats of naked, shackled men; giant leather-strapped penises and men being fucked with crucifixes; queens cackling and trannies flicking their feather boas and sequins in her eye—and it was nothing like the gender theory she'd studied at uni, with its reassuring sense of empowerment, nothing like the safe dipping into language in the privacy of her girlhood bedroom. Two groups seemed to form—male and female snaking their way through Darlinghurst and then separating, as couples do at a midsummer night's barbecue. Leonie broke away, leaving the glitter and tinsel behind, and was followed by a woman who looked like a man, with stringy hair and blackened, broken toenails. Leonie quickened her pace, tried to shake her off like an unwanted dog, but the woman followed her all the way to the botanical gardens, seemed to wait for her in the shadows there.

And what to tell the young man now? Those brief years of study that are lost to the realities of a working life, the real world where people aren't reading the same books, talking the same political discourse, and eventually you find yourself, as a rubber band does, pinging back in size. And then gradually, over time, Leonie took on the shape of her mother, with all the same prejudices, the same foolish desires; the pull of the catechism, hair cut like English thatch and a body thickened with the approach of menopause—in her case, hastened by surgery and the clinical skill of her surgeon. A surgeon who looked years younger than Leonie, and dressed as if he should be seeing a better class of patient. That first day she visited his rooms, she waited for over an hour with five other women, reading their magazines and whispering their annoyance to their husbands. When her name was called—*Ms Taylor*—the surgeon didn't know what to do with the Ms, made it buzz like a piece of onomatopoeia stuck in his throat. Leonie was there for only five minutes, but that was enough time for her to see his freshly scrubbed cuticles and the framed degree from the University of Sydney on his wall, and for him to draw a picture of a uterus and hand it to her: a sketch of an inverted pear on a piece of paper. Later, she had laughed about it with her mother, saying, 'Things are really going pear-shaped.'

Yes, she thought now. That was the shape of things to come.

\* \* \*

Leonie woke through a medicated fog, tried to wade past the thick tribal beat three floors above, to get to the other sound, a different sound: the brittleness of something trying to break through, rattling at the window, splintering the wood. Shit, an intruder. She edged her way in the dark towards the door of her bedroom, her hand searching for the switch. The light made no difference; whoever it was remained bold and didn't scuttle away like a roach.

'I've called the cops,' she shouted out.

This time there was a slowing of the sound, a clumsy retreat. Leonie peered out the curtains and saw the shadowy blue of figures dissolving into the night.

'What's wrong?' The young man lay on the couch, looking alert and fresh.

'Didn't you hear the men trying to get in?'

'I heard nothing.'

'I'll wait up. See if they come back.' She turned off the light and sat in the armchair next to him, until eventually she could hear his soft breaths convert into something heavier. In the morning, her neck was sore from where her head had jerked into and out of sleep.

Not long to go now, she thought, and this craziness will be over. She padded into the kitchen, not wanting to disturb the sleeping figure. She usually had cold cereal for breakfast, but today she was going to cook something heartier—throw caution to the wind, as her mother would say. What did it matter about the extra calories? She knew she would become fat like a spayed labrador regardless. When she had finished cooking, she carried the plates of chipolata, eggs and Swiss mushrooms out to the living room and sat on the couch next to him, bringing him alive with the savoury aroma. Not exactly a date, but Leonie preferred it this way, sitting side by side. The way men like to bond at the footy.

'Are you sure you don't want to see a doctor?'

'I'm fine.'

She nodded and felt the happiness flutter through her body.

'We could watch a movie,' Leonie suggested, and the young man looked at her, through those pale, pellucid eyes, neither agreeing nor disagreeing.

She rummaged in the entertainment unit, trying to find something he might enjoy. There wasn't a lot of choice. It was obvious when she had stopped bothering to buy DVDs, and she hovered between *Four Weddings and a Funeral* and *Groundhog Day*. They ended up watching both. She felt her headache return: a spacey, guilty feeling of watching daytime movies when you should be outside in the sun.

About four o'clock the music started up again (why so early?), and the fear flowed through her in cold, undulating waves. She thought about cooking. Turned on the whirring fan above the electric stove, clanged pots and pans, just to drown out the growing beat. The young man followed her into the kitchen.

'Is it okay for me to have a shower?'

'Of course. Of course.'

Leonie hurried to the bathroom and found a box of guest soaps that her mother had given her one Christmas, their pink corners powdered and crumbling, and the towel that felt least like dried-out cardboard. She waited for him to finish, the sound of the water barely covering the shrieks and caterwauling, and the unrelenting dance party music building to a crescendo. Soon the noise would get too loud to bear and she would stand and look at the men gathering outside. Through the curtains she could see them move in a concerted blur, but occasionally she made out a bald head amongst the crowd.

When the young man finally stepped into the room, a fine mist from the shower seemed to come with him, and when it cleared Leonie gasped at the vision: glistening bare chest, silky white boxers, and rising from his shoulders two magnificent tessellated wings.

Was it really the Archangel Michael, sent as both avenger and judge to smite this city? But before she could ask, he had opened the door and slipped away into the crowd that was moving as one growing organism down the dank streets, past all the narrow terraces with their boxy rooms, down to Oxford Street, dirty Oxford Street, to the place where the procession always begins. Leonie tried to follow, to search him out in the pulsating throng, but there were hundreds of angels now, all beautiful and near naked, except for their little silky boxer shorts, and it was impossible to tell one from the other.

## THE SHAPE OF THINGS

Leonie felt her head pounding, the red cells glowing and about to explode, and held her hand against a building to steady herself. She could see it was the solid white façade of the Jewish Museum, its column strangely cool and comforting. She remembered coming here a year ago with her mother after a long, indulgent lunch, where they had both been invisible to the beautiful waiters, and her mother had to force strength into her thin, reedy voice so they would hear her words over the jangling trays. The museum was a whim, something to stave off returning to their lonely, separate lives, so they walked in on this odd collection of random, stand-alone relics. And there was one exhibit that had caught and held Leonie's eye, one exhibit that seemed to make all the difference: a single rubber boot recovered from a mass grave in Sernik—and it was collapsing in on itself, losing whatever shape it kept before. The sort of thing that can make you cry.

Tonight the museum was closed; all was quiet and dignified and white except for the hot-pink poster gashing the wall. *A pink triangle trapped in a green circle*. Leonie noticed a trail of them leading down the street, pasted on every wall and shop front, stretching further than the eye could see. So she decided to follow the posters to their natural beginning (or was it their conclusion?), hoping to spot more outposts of geometry and colour, wishing to find the girl from the laundromat so she could tell her that two triangles can, possibly, make a star.

# DYING

Someone gave her a copy of the book *Crazy Sexy Cancer Survivor* and she only had to read the blurb at the back to know it wasn't for her. It was written for younger women with blonde hair, straightened teeth and breasts. Both of her breasts had been removed by a surgeon wearing a green fabric mask who played water polo on Thursdays. Her chest resembled a map from a war zone, rumpled and worn.

At the district hospital she had her wound checked by a nurse from Zimbabwe. The nurse's hair was braided in tight whorls knitted to her head, and her skin was so black that her features were indiscernible, her face unknowable. The nurse didn't talk much, gave nothing of herself away, but later she could hear the way the woman's voice came alive as she joked with an elderly man behind the next curtain, as she repeated the banter that nurses reserve for favourite patients. Just not for her.

When her husband drove her back to the farm, there was no need to talk; they had the Country Hour to listen to and they could watch the wheaten patterns race by in the half-light and flicker over their faces like an old silent movie. Returning to the farmhouse was like returning to the scene of a crime. This is where she had found the lump, buried pea-deep beneath her skin.

\*\*\*

The worst bit about having cancer was the life she would leave behind. Her children were away at boarding school, and even though they had learned to be independent and relied on others for daily advice, she worried about who would sew the endless name tags on their clothing and send them the novelty birthday cakes and care packages. When she spoke to them on the phone she made her voice sound strong and unbreakable; it was easy to be a disembodied mother voice. What was hard was trying to imagine life beyond this time, how they would look as adults when they lost the round cheeks of their youth and were whittled into older versions of themselves. She searched the Internet for a website for mothers with cancer, for mothers who could post a picture of a teenager and have it magically transform into a middle-aged son, a pregnant daughter. All she could find was a site on how to convert yourself into a blue-skinned creature from *Avatar*.

There was still so much that she needed to tell them about life. She wanted to write it all down, make them a list called 'Advice for Living', so they would always have that wise mother voice forever funnelled down a crackling landline, telling them things like 'Too much eyeliner makes you look cheap' and 'You lose a little of yourself each time you fall in love'.

\* \* \*

She had first met her husband at youth group. Fell off his lap during a game of Knights, Horses and Cavaliers, and saw how the embarrassment flushed the sides of his face and prickled his neck like a rash. She noticed every small detail. The way he would stand one step back from the others; the way he let his eyes follow her every small flirtation around the room. She knew he had marked her out from the very beginning, but she had her own crushes to pursue, and years later, after they had played out in fitful bursts, she was left standing with him alone by his father's ute. She liked the taste of him when they kissed long and hard. And she liked how he absorbed her energy and glanced across for help when stranded in a circle of strangers.

After they married, they were given a small workman's cottage to live in whilst his parents remained in the bigger, more comfortable house. She quickly made the cottage into a home. She found an odd assortment of second-hand furniture, restored an old 1950s kitchenette with yellow and green paint, re-covered a fading sofa in calico, and salvaged ceramic and iron bed knobs from a neighbour's yard. She trawled magazines for recipes and got ideas from her girlfriends, now living and working in the city. After seven nights of eating Apricot Chicken, her husband had quietly said, *I think we need to have something else for dinner*.

Summers were hot, and she had to learn to recycle grey water from the laundry trough onto the veggie patch out the back. She had begged for a small patch of lawn, insisted on it for their future children. Water was pumped up from the front dam, and by the end of March there was a thick slick of mud shining like scales between the tough runners of buffalo. She watched the dragonflies dangle and dart, and the pink and grey cockatoos shuffle across the lawn like returned soldiers.

Each season they seemed to scrape by, and soon the wool cheque was set aside for school fees and for doing up the larger house, when succession plans were finally made. She can't remember the year when the freshwater soak became too salty, and the majestic river gums died back into a line of ghostly limbs. Or the year when the marron marched across the paddocks and her children collected them in pails like precious coins. All the while the land was on its downward struggle, her little death seed must have been slowly, silently growing.

\* \* \*

The thing about cancer is that everyone wants to give you a piece of hope. *Here, take this*, they say, and it hovers over you like a gentle brown-winged creature. Friends left her books about juicing, pamphlets about meditation and healing retreats, and added her to their prayer chains. Living became more exhausting than dying as she felt the pressure from others to put up a good fight.

She wished she had that sinew of tenacity, could stretch out her bony fingers and hang on for dear life—just like the orphaned lambs, when she'd held them on her knee and willed them to drink. The lambs would at first refuse; she had to stroke their chins and slip and slide the rubbery teat into their mouths. But once the animal tasted the warm, frothy milk, it would tug at the bottle and pull so hard that she could feel the power in its jaw, the resolve rippling down its neck. Her own children didn't feed like this; they were fed on demand, and took their time grazing and nibbling at her breast, before she finally plucked them from her nipple like fat buds.

Her body was too weak to fight. She had lost so much weight that her jeans hung from her hips. Maybe that was another thing she could add to her 'Advice for Living' list: 'There is such a thing as too skinny'. She lost her hair, her eyebrows, her lashes. She thought she resembled an egg. *No need to get a Brazilian*, she laughed with her friends. She didn't tell them that her labia, so droopy and exposed, looked like a collapsed flower.

* * *

When you are sick, reading becomes too difficult. Not just the weight of the book, or the words that shift and dance before your eyes: without a sense of a future, there's no desire to turn the pages. That's why she relied on the television to fill her days, to allow the endless loop of shows to buffer her from the spreading boredom.

She tried to sort out her cupboards, fuelled by the desire to have her life neatened and organised so that even strangers would later marvel at how clean she was. In her dining room cabinet she found all the precious things kept aside for special occasions: cake servers still in their original gift boxes, the Noritake wedding crockery, champagne flutes, an unburned pink-petalled candle. Another thing to tell her children: 'Never wait for special occasions'. She found old boxes of 21st birthday cards, and cards from friends she hadn't seen for years, with those funny comments that now made no sense, being long removed from the source. 'Absence does not make the heart grow fonder'.

She couldn't bear to think of Christmas, when those glittery green Seasons Greetings would begin to pile up on the kitchen table. She snapped at her husband when he tried to discuss plans about planting drought-resistant tagasaste, or wondered whether spring lambs would reach $100 a head.

At night they slept in separate bedrooms, and when she couldn't sleep, she roamed the house like an unwelcome guest. She opened and closed the fridge, unable to decide how to cut the nausea that rose hotly from her belly. Strawberries had the right acidity, but black tea was astringent, more like a remedy. Summer nights melded into days. She wore the same cotton nightie, and sweated into the fabric while her husband walked the boundary fences. She learned how to chase her pain, dip under it and fly beside it until it fitted her body perfectly.

Once she came to his bed, crept between the covers without saying a word. She wanted to feel his hands on her body, feel that desire in his mouth, and have it cover her entire skin. But she was too brittle. She could come apart in his hands. It seemed there was nothing left of her for him to touch or to hold.

She whispered, 'Graham, I think you should remarry.'

'Not this,' he answered, letting his hand lightly tremble at her shoulders.

\* \* \*

'It can be disappointing to return to the place you once lived'. She needed to tell her children that. The house will look smaller than how they wished to remember it, and shabbier, like their old ginger cat with its half-licked fur. It will have an echo, like those holiday places people pass by on the way to somewhere better. This was how it was with the old workman's cottage, their first home now set up as shearers' short-term accommodation. She walked around the yard like a puppet in her boots, picking up one foot after the other to pull herself over the sods of earth. The garden had died back to a rough border of natives, except for a leggy pelargonium. Everywhere, it seemed as if the world was shrinking away from her: lizards rustled under leaves, birds startled away from the fence. She walked to the edge of the garden bed, where the outside bath-tub was once hidden under a private bower of green. Their secret retreat from the world of farming, from her husband's family popping over unannounced. This is where she laughed as her husband poured water down her back, and then, as she settled into their nakedness, allowed him to slip on top of her in the tub, so that her breasts were pressed out, floating like white buoys on the water.

She could imagine the woman he would eventually come to marry. Someone he could slip easily on to, into.

\* \* \*

'Morphine can make dying a beautiful thing'. She began to slowly unfold. She lay on the hospital bed and listened to the world vibrate: the metal instruments on the trolley tray, the rustle of the plastic sheet beneath her, the tractor's hum in the treeless distance. Someone put a sponge in her mouth and it tasted of the laundry trough. Her mouth was now a desert cave. She thought she spoke out loud, Can I go swimming? and a cool black hand came to rest an answer on her brow. She dreamed of a green, clear lake. A lake that freezes over in winter. She had once read about fishermen in Minnesota using ice augers to cut rough holes in the thick ice, dropping simple lines into the waters full of bream and walleyed pike.

*Imagine if someone fell through the ice and couldn't find their way back*, she had told her husband, frightened by the thought of someone like a small child being trapped under an immovable weight.

*It wouldn't matter*, he replied. *The cold would kill them outright.*

But it seemed as if he was wrong all along. First, there is the head-over-heels surprise and plummet, falling through chinks of chill-green; then the descent into the deepest waters. And the temperatures were after all bearable. Survivable. She swam the length of the whole world under this great expanse of ice, dipping in and out of air pockets like a white-skinned porpoise, trying to find its way back to the pod.

# HAPPY DAYS

*Six Degrees*

That's the textbook angle for getting a strike, according to the Australian Federation of Bowling. It's all in the way you curve your wrist, arcing the ball towards that magic place between the centre pin and the one to the right. One two three four steps as you enter the approach then release the ball, almost touching the white clasp of your ankle-bone.

Ollie tries to do this; I can see him closing his eyes as he visualises that moment when everything finally lines up: his body, his mind, the planets. But he falters at the line, loses his courage, does a strange twisting motion with his wrist and gets the dreaded 7–10 split.

It's Monday night league and I'm minding the kiosk again. Technically I should be home studying for my Year Ten exams, but Ollie is really good at getting his own way. *Hey Josh, you don't mind, do you? Letting your ol' uncle have a chance to unwind?* If he unwound any more, he'd be lying on the floor.

When Ollie first decided to have a go at bowling he joined the only team who would take on the risk: The Ebowlas. Ollie was convinced he could still run the kiosk and play at the same time. But this league eats and drinks the most out of all of them. I should know: I spend the night running back and forth to the fridge, to the fryer, to the counter, moving faster than the balls themselves.

I shouldn't complain. Each league has a particular vibe, and this one is probably the best of the lot. The bowlers are less worn out, have a particular upswing in their step, unlike the Wednesday night bowlers with their droopy, sad bums. It's those bums that I always remember. Monday night puckered apples, or flat, drop-down-to-the-ocean Wednesday ones.

The lanes are roaring fast—there is a rumbling energy like rush hour at the train station as the balls thunder down the polished wood and crash into the pins, and then the *clickety clack* return of the ball, a never-ending smash-and-crash cycle. I swear I'm going deaf: there's no escaping the noise of the balls, the flying pins, the excitable, superimposed chatter. It's impossible to study so I decide to redo the Specials board, try and make a difference with some coloured chalk. It's been the same 'Special' for weeks now: Happy Days Chilli Dog, which is really just a hotdog with a squirt of Heinz chilli sauce. Happy Days Café—that's the name Ollie came up with as he tried to rebrand the kiosk with a retro fifties theme. He bought some vintage Coca-Cola mirrors from an auction and tore out some pages from an old calendar featuring women wearing frilly aprons, pearls and frosted smiles. The pictures are pasted around the walls above the prep area, some tatty at the edges and spattered with brown gobs of oil, and it has the grubby look of a teenager's room from the fifties. It doesn't work—but then it doesn't matter what Ollie does because the rest of the bowl will always be a dump. Things are beyond his control: the dandelions sprouting like triffids from the potholes in the car park, the battered balls and shoes which haven't been replaced for years, and the dated electronic scoring system from the nineties with the flashing animations of a fox going *Kapow!* every time there is a strike.

There has been talk of a buy-out lately, something about the AMF wanting to take over one of the last independent bowling alleys left in Perth, but this is only a ten-lane affair and you need at least fourteen lanes to make a go of it. Gary neither confirms nor denies the rumour. I hate his guts. Not just the way he has lied to Ollie about the business, locking him into an up-front seven-year lease, but how whenever he sees Ollie walking towards him he takes out his iPhone and pretends to be deep in conversation. And then there are the times he collects the change from the pinnies and the ball polishing machine, and the sound of falling coins reverberates through the building, giving everyone a false sense of hope.

Gary owns the bowl and has the easy-to-stretch smile of a con man. He still has the ponytail from the days when he worked as a bouncer at Pinocchio's Night Club, and twenty kilos later there he sits in the side office, the tattoos swelling like monsoons on his forearms as he stuffs the week's takings from the safe into cream calico bags. Lee, his offsider, works beside him and they've always got their heads bowed together as if they're conjoined twins.

I watch Ollie and he's trying to fit in with the other bowlers. He's doing something weird with his lips, testing out a smile and showing too much gum like a mare. I recognise it because Mum does the same thing when she's around people she's not sure of. Smiling and all gums, and everyone thinking she is really nice when in fact she just has low self-esteem. It reminds me of the time when I was eight, and Ollie and I were walking through the bush on one of our prospecting trips and we found a stray dog. Its brown mangy fur was missing in patches and its ribs radiated out through the skin like the blue whale skeleton at the museum. It was covered with kangaroo ticks, black and plump. *Riddled*, Mum said, and that word sounded so thrilling to me because gangster bodies were always riddled with bullets. But she wouldn't let us keep it, organised for the council ranger to come and collect it from our laundry the next day. The dog's eyes were filmy and yellow like a lizard's, and when I stared into them to communicate my love for it, to let the dog know how much I cared, its lip curled back from its teeth in a soundless warning. I find myself doing the same thing when Gary comes to the counter, his hair greasier and more grown out than usual. I'm baring my teeth in an all-gum smile. It's a warning, the kind given by cornered prey: You better back off, or else.

## *Doing an Andy Varipapa*

It's not impossible when you have a 7–10 split, if you put enough spin on the ball so that the power and force ricochets one pin across the deck, to collect the remaining one on the other side. I know that Ollie is going for it but I can't bear to watch, so I pretend to be rearranging the pyrex cups stacked on top of the coffee machine. There is a roar from the bowlers and I know he has failed.

When Ollie first took over the kiosk he would invite me over to his place in Kelmscott, a small boxy unit in a large group near the railway line, and I would weave my way past the bundles of newspapers, the boxes from the blind auctions, and sit in a small clearing he had made in the kitchen, where we would watch old black and white newsreels of Andy Varipapa. *Papa Varipapa*—looking more like a Brooklyn pizza parlour owner than a two-time All-Star American champ. Ollie would replay the famous tricks: the scatter shot, the drop kick, the double hook, the bank shot, and my personal favourite, the Sunday driver—where Ollie and I would laugh more at the American voice-over than the erratic ball:

*A fellow drives all over the road, even on the left-hand side.* The man's voice was old-fashioned and measured and I felt like I was watching something of historical importance, like a space mission. We sometimes ate while we watched, putting our plates on one of Ollie's many boxes, and the heat would soften and buckle the cardboard. Sometimes I feared our food would disappear, like cars falling through the earth's crust during an earthquake. Ollie was the happiest during those times. His eyes would fixate on the replay of the shots, and the superimposed lines that tracked the pathway of the ball, revealing the hidden mystery. *It's all to do with physics*, Ollie would say, and I would nod and remember to pay more attention during Mr Przywolniek's science class at school.

It was the same happiness Ollie had when talking about the ring. The Andy Varipapa commemorative ring for the perfect 300. Twelve consecutive strikes over two games. No-one at the bowl had ever got one, and Ollie became obsessed with checking fingers if anyone new joined his league. I found myself doing the same thing. Whenever a customer came to the counter I would do a quick once-over of their hands, hold my breath whenever a ring was squarish and chunkier than usual. Sometimes I would do a voice-over in my head: A fellow comes to the counter and is wearing a ring. It's chunky and gold, and there could be a number 300 in black lettering with a little chip of diamanté, but—wait, folks… no need for concern: it's just a skull and crossbones set!

## *Dead Wood, Dead Wood*

Lee calls it out over the PA system, and I look up to see that Ollie's attempt at the 7–10 split has left a remaining pin on the laneway, which the mechanical arm has failed to sweep away. Ollie starts walking down the lane, lightly pressing his bowling shoes on the polished wood as if trying not to leave imprints on wet cement, and then Lee's voice booms out like an angry god. 'Get off the fuckin' lane, Ollie.'

All the other bowlers titter and grin, and Ollie slips and slides as he starts running back. I can see that Lee's latest girlfriend has brought in bags of Chinese takeaway and has spread out the containers on the console like a picnic. I strain to see whether there are bottles of Coke as well. I have suspected for a while now that Lee has been nicking the buddy bottles from our fridge—he always denies it, but I sometimes see him slipping something beneath his flannel shirt, and whenever I walk over to check the bookings diary to see whether there are any birthday parties lined up for the weekend, there are telltale damp circles on the open pages.

Lee's girlfriend is wearing a lime-green midriff top and her belly button piercing sticks out like the ring top from a can. She reluctantly lifts up the hinged flap of the console, so Lee can walk along the back of the lanes to sweep away the stranded pin with a broom. At most I give this relationship four weeks. Lee's relationships are getting shorter and shorter and I think it's because the bowl no longer has the pull it used to. Being an average-looking guy with a set of alley keys isn't enough any more, but he reeled her in, in the way he always does with his girlfriends. He led her by the hand over to the ball racks, whispering, *You need a ball about a tenth of your body weight*, let his eyes slowly travel the length of her body, then picked out a shiny five-kilo Black Beauty. And she was hooked.

Lee has been working at the bowl for years, and before that his dad worked there in the glory days when it used to be a carpet warehouse. One time when I couldn't find Lee and Gary at the front desk, I wandered down the back end, past the dust-coated crap: old balls chipped like moon craters, oily rags, bolts and crank handles rusted in one-arm salutes, and the broken fifties-style monitors with their grey outer-space hoods. It was like entering another world, and as I went deeper into the darkness, imagining I was a deep-sea diver in the murky unfathomable depths of the ocean where only bottom feeders lurk, my eyes suddenly adjusted and I saw the huge rolls of industrial carpet stacked high to the ceiling like limp bodies. I never told Ollie this because I know he'll want to go down the back to check out all the junk for himself.

In real life Lee's voice sounds weak and reedy, but over the PA system it transforms into something deeper, like the wizard in the movie *The Wizard of Oz*, though whenever he says a word beginning with a 'p' it sounds all girly again, a tiny marshmallow *pouff*. I would like to hear him say 'Papa Varipapa'. He's quieter during the league, but on a Saturday evening when it's Rock 'n' Bowl Lee doesn't stop talking, as if he is a radio DJ and everyone has turned up just to listen to him. His one true gift, though, is matching the music to the bowlers, choosing the Rolling Stones when the Baby Boomers come in for a social game, Taylor Swift for the ten-year-old girls' parties, and for the local footy club wind-up—his own personal favourite, 'Fun with Farts'.

Some weekends it's only him and me; Ollie hasn't turned up, there are no bowlers and we are in our separate zones on opposite sides of the room. All we can hear, while we stand there eyeing each other off in silence, is the dull sound of a drill from the back lots pushing its way into the empty space. There was this one time though on a Sunday afternoon, only a single lane going, and the glass doors suddenly swung open and a group of hipsters walked in and it was like an alien invasion—the guys with gingery-brown bushy beards and wearing skinny jeans and bomber jackets, the girls dressed in skater skirts with pastel-coloured shirts knotted in at their waists. They circumnavigated the bowl, checking out everything with knowing looks, giggling like Japanese schoolgirls beneath their palms. And when they finally left without playing a single game Lee turned on his microphone, spat out the word *Wankers!* And that was the only time I ever came close to liking him.

## *FLO*

Most of the league bowlers have their FLO—a habit, a ritual, a superstitious set of tics or dance moves they have to complete before a game. Some cross themselves, kiss a stuffed toy, or in Ollie's case, rub the glossy folds of Buddha's belly. Between his games Ollie comes over to the counter to recharge his luck on the Buddha we have standing on the counter next to the straw dispenser. He is proud of that golden statue (the best thing he has ever got at an auction), and its shiny, chuckling face is so different from the concrete one with the formless features in the garden, the one Mum bought as a reminder of a holiday in Bali—though I hate to be the one to tell her that Bali's a predominately Hindu island.

'How much have we taken tonight, Josh?' Ollie asks me, and I have to go through the motions of doing a till read-out because Ollie has this constant need to check how much money he has made. I used to love doing this too, turning the key on the cash register, pressing the button and watching the docket spit out its inky purple running tally for the day. I don't want to tell Ollie that it's probably only fifteen dollars, but then luckily Dallas comes to the counter to order her own FLO, a large basket of chips with gravy, and Ollie forgets about the read-out and seems happy again. I turn the fryer up to 180 degrees and go into the small kitchen annexe to get the frozen chips. The coffin freezer is almost empty except for a box of squid rings and a handful of loose chips which have melded into the icy bottom, so I pry them off with a knife and put them into the wire basket for frying. It's so embarrassing. Ollie hasn't done a shop in ages, but at least we still have the ginormous tin of instant gravy that we bought from Foodland Cash and Carry, the warehouse wonderland. You can only shop at Foodland Cash and Carry if you have proof you own a business, and in Ollie's case it's having his own ABN. The first time Ollie and I went shopping there, we were like little elves looking up at the giant shelves of jumbo-sized everything: tomato sauce, mustard, sacks of sugar, flour, rice and plastic spoons. Everything economical and in bulk. We went crazy during that first shop, even adding giant bags of lollies—milk bottles, musk sticks, snakes, teeth, sour worms—that Ollie was going to make up into lucky dips. We circled the warehouse with our two trolleys, looking at the other customers and trying to suss them out: the hamburger joint owner with his super-sized tubs of mayo; the not-for-profit holiday church groups with their forty loaves of white bread; and the mothers in loose shorts and flip-flops, their cracked heels a floury-grey colour, making us wonder, did you really need an ABN to shop at Foodland Cash and Carry? And there is something about jumbo-sized things that makes you feel tired, saps all the energy out of your dwarfish legs. We loaded up the car and I felt drained and blah, that same kind of feeling I get when shopping for Back to School supplies with Mum.

When the food is finally ready I take it out to Dallas. She is standing at the counter with Ollie, having a conversation of sorts without facing him. Dallas, bigger than the State of Texas, wearing her signature muumuu dress with white bobby socks and red bowling shoes. I explain to her that I don't have enough chips but have given her a complimentary serve of squid rings to make up for it. Squid rings and chips are not her FLO, but she doesn't complain because she knows that squid rings are the most expensive item on the menu. Ollie looks a little peeved, but then I realise he is waiting for something else. *Happy Days*. He has instructed me to say these magic words every time a customer receives their order, but I can never bring myself to do it. It sounds too naff. I prefer to say *Cheers*— short and abrupt yet breezy friendly. But Ollie is watching me and I can see he is moving his lips slightly, pre-empting the words like he does when watching a favourite movie. So Dallas stands there heavily shaking the chicken salt all over her complimentary squid and chips and I start to speak, then lose my nerve and the words come out in a quick tumble, sounding something more like 'happy ears'.

## *Gutter Ball*

Ollie's next shot for the night trickles down the channel without collecting a single pin. Strictly speaking it should be called a channel ball but the word 'gutter' punches at the heart more. I watch the replay on the video monitor, the cheesy animation of a little pig crying *wee wee wee* all the way home. That's the worst thing with the video screen—your humiliation plays out in animal form. Ollie makes a joke of it and gives a little shrug. That's Ollie's way of dealing with disappointment—a shrug or a plan. He is always coming up with a new scheme to make this shithole work. Pizza 'n' Bowl—install a wood-fired pizza oven, and make some dough outta dough! Drive-Thru Bowl— knock a window through to the car park for those who want takeaway without setting a foot inside. And some of his ideas aren't that crazy. Almost doable. One time he asked Gary if he could convert the crèche into a birthday party room so he could have multiple birthday parties booked at the same time, instead of trying to cram all the kids onto the plastic tables at the front of the counter. This crèche is a complete disaster, a narrow, dark room filled with old school desks and dirty toys: baby rattles, stackable plastic ring sets with only one ring left, used colouring-in books, and naked Barbie dolls, their faces scrawled with blue biro. No-one ever uses this room except for a couple of single mothers from the team Alley Cats on the Wednesday night league. But Gary refused, forcing Ollie to come up with even more outrageous ideas. He thought about converting old car bodies into table booths to fit in with the *Happy Days* theme, but when he asked Mum if he could store the wrecks on her back lawn, she simply said, *Oh, Ollie.*

It's not that Mum isn't supportive. It was her idea to let her brother move in with us shortly after Dad died. Ollie was given the spare room, but soon he'd taken over the shed and the conversation pit began to fill up with boxes. Then there were the wings of a glider kit which he left out on the buffalo lawn, the silver streaks being slowly eaten by runners of green. Eventually Mum told him it was time to move on and found him the small unit, and it was sad to see all the stuff go. And even now when I go into the spare room and open the cupboard where a few of Dad's old shirts are still stored, I can't tell if it's Ollie's smell or Dad's that returns like the infilling of the Holy Spirit after Mum does a quick once-over with a can of Glen 20.

## *A Turkey*

On the monitor I can see a turkey with a thanksgiving tail strutting down the lanes proudly, and I wish it was Ollie who'd got the three consecutive strikes in a row. Ollie loves this turkey animation—maybe that's why he was chuffed when he dreamed up 'Turkey 'n' Bowl', a way to cash in on the Christmas in July phenomena.

He convinced Mum to hold the teachers' annual Christmas party at the bowling alley even though they had their hearts set on a Miss Maud's all you can eat smorgasbord. Mum allowed me to sleep over at Ollie's the night before so I could help with all the prep. In the morning I found him dunking a frozen turkey in a sink of hot water. It was too late to defrost and cook it in time, so Ollie ended up going to Chicken Treat and buying eight cooked chooks to make into platters, along with iceberg lettuce and carrot sticks. He had spent the previous night peeling bags of potatoes. 'No-one can say I'm stingy,' he boasted, proudly covering them with a drum-tight layer of gladwrap before putting them in the car.

When we arrived at the bowl, we set up quickly, me putting bits of gold tinsel over the monitors and red plastic cloths over the tables while Ollie started deep-frying the potatoes whole. Then he loaded the bain-marie with mountains of spuds, and one tray with gravy, which he'd mixed from the tin.

Mum was the first to arrive. She carried in the Secret Santa gifts and, as if on cue, Lee put on the Michael Bublé Christmas CD. Mum looked tired but happy, wore her favourite floaty, peacock-blue blouse and had a bounce in her step in time with the music. Then she saw the chicken platters, the potatoes in the bain-marie. 'Are they roasted?' she asked, and when I told her they were deep-fried she frowned, saying, 'Are you sure you can cook them like that?' I, too, had my doubts but wasn't going to tell her.

Soon the place filled up with teachers, and it had the smug buzz of a quiz night. Lee lined up the battered red-and-white bowling shoes on the counter, their tongues hanging out like panting dogs, and he sprayed a large green can of deodorant back and forth over them. The teachers picked through the items as if they were choosing the least damaged fruit at the market. Mum looked frazzled. Entrées were meant to be served before the first game, and afterwards, mains followed by dessert. I raced around with the dips still in their containers and the packet of Ritz for dunking. Ollie followed behind with the olives. I recognised lots of faces and they all wanted to ask me questions. There was Mrs Johnson, the music teacher who had known Mum for ages, wearing flashing reindeer earrings; Miss Lewis, a leathery, shrivelled-up sports teacher who'd spent a lot of time chasing balls in the sun; and Mr Sims, the bearded chemistry teacher, who walked as if he has a rod up his bum. I weaved my dips through the group, giving out as much information as it takes to scoop some hummus onto a cracker. For once I didn't mind that Mum had shared so much of my life with them. It might just get us over the line.

At twelve, the teachers all lined up for the buffet, full of expectations, picked over the chicken and left the mound of potatoes. There was a sombre mood in the room—it was the sound of no-one eating—but the Coles pavlovas were perking Ollie up. He dolloped cream and piled strawberries and kiwi fruit on top. *Everyone loves a pav!* (Not if they thought they were getting trifle.)

But the final straw was the coffee. People can put up with bad food, but when you're paying top dollar, your cappuccino cannot be Nescafé instant with whipped froth on top.

The deputy principal, Sue McGurk, had put her shoes back on, become the leaning tower of Pisa again, and her heels rasped and snagged across the thin industrial carpet as she approached our counter.

'I'll have a flat white.'

Ollie looked confused.

'You do know what a flat white is?' she said, as she adjusted her tortoiseshell bifocals to examine the chalkboard menu, to take it all in.

'Cappuccino,' Ollie replied, and handed her the instant coffee topped with an eggy white cloud.

And that was the beginning of the end.

## *Wombat*

That's what you call it when you throw a spare after a gutter ball. Ollie's last ball of the night is a wombat and he dances around on the 'approach', high-fiving his other team members. I almost think he is going to attempt a click of the heels like Andy Varipapa does in the old movies. Everyone starts huddling in for the final debrief and review of the leader board, and I know I have about fifteen minutes to do a quick mop of the floor and count the money before the bowlers start grabbing their stuff and exiting to the car park.

I look across to the other side of the room and see that Lee and Gary already have their heads bowed together as they do their own till count, their fingers trilling over the paper bills. The first time I saw them count their money I was secretly pleased to see that they weren't as quick as Ollie. Ollie's first job was in a bank, in the days you could leave school in Year Ten with an achievement certificate, and I could imagine his chubby face at fifteen peering through a glass window at the line of customers. Even though Ollie is almost fifty, and grizzled around his temple with a harvest crop of stubble on his chin, there is still a round schoolboy softness about his face. And he has the bluest eyes, the kind of blue I always associate with clear skies and open doorways. I don't know what happened at the bank, maybe it had something to do with the nervous breakdown that Mum hints at, but I sometimes see it when he zones in and out of conversations, or in the involuntary muscle spasm beneath his right eye, like a tiny tremor along a dangerous fault line.

I am squeezing out the mop head—a grey trickle of water oozes out, into my bucket—and Ollie comes over and bangs his bowling bag onto the counter.

'Super sippers,' he blurts out. 'You fill these cups with postmix and give a refill for half price. If we water down the second lot of syrup no-one will ever know. The law of diminishing returns, right?' He smiles at me. 'The second bite is never as good as the first!'

I stare at him dumbly, wondering what on earth he is on about, but before I can answer Gary comes up to the kiosk, the smirk on his lips twisting into a Joker-like grin.

'I was thinking, Ollie. We'll have to add an extra tariff to your electricity bill. You know, the carbon tax and all.'

As he is saying this, Gary presses down on the silver straw dispenser, a pad-like movement with his fingertip, and a straw neatly rolls out into the depository. He fishes it out with his fat finger and thumb, and twirls it around like a swizzle stick. I stare at Gary's dirty fingernails and funnel as much hate as I can muster into the fingertips, down the straw hole and into his greasy, black heart. I glance across at Ollie, but he doesn't look any different. Maybe there is the slightest movement beneath his right eye like the pulse of a tiny sparrow, but his clear blue eyes are staring ahead at the video monitor, which has gone into its usual default image of a desert island. There's a sandy beach, a single palm tree, and the bluest water stretching out to a winking horizon. And I too stare at that screen, so that my eyes begin to do strange things with the pixelated dots and colours of the sand, the tree, the water, the sky. They start to blur and move together, in the same way that when you stare long enough at a whiteboard full of mathematical equations the numbers begin to sway and dance and join hands with one another, not unlike a never-ending chorus line of paper-chain children.

# FABULOUS LIVES

It was too late for Edith. She knew that when she stood in the lobby of 11 Howard Street staring at the warehouse-sized sterile room, empty except for a central round table with an iPad plonked in the middle. Ricky had organised this SoHo hotel for her and she wondered if it was intentional, to suggest a place where she was clearly not the intended demographic. At forty-eight, she was the oldest guest here, though it was difficult to tell the customers and hotel staff apart—everyone wore the same stock-standard uniform of dark hoodies and designer ripped jeans.

Edith felt wearied from the long journey from Australia and thankful that Ricky kept cancelling on her. He was held up in meetings with his agent, and then there was the situation with another acting friend. *You know the type, Edith. Real drama queen.*

So she spent the first few days on her own, walking the streets of SoHo and then visiting all the landmark buildings—the Empire State Building, the Rockefeller Center, Grand Central Station. And it was quite surreal. She would have this sudden flash of familiarity—a sense of déjà vu, as if she had been here before—and then the frustration would take over as she pushed her pitiful brain to nut out exactly which movie scene she was remembering. In this way Edith never felt fully present, push-pulling her brain for a slice of *something*, so that the whole experience became dissatisfying and exhausting. Central Park was different though. She stood on the outer fringe of the park, saw the leafless, barely-alive trees, and the horses shivering and exhaling puffs of air like dragons, and thought dispassionately, this moment belongs only to me. It didn't last. It was too cold to stand outside—her Perth-bought coat clearly inadequate for a New York winter—so she crossed over the street and went to find refuge in an Italian-style restaurant.

The cheeriness of the place instantly lifted Edith's spirits. Big brass lamps glowed and candles flickered light into all the dark recesses, and the young waiters had a healthy sheen to their skin that suggested long summers in faraway places. She was shown a table one back from the window, so the only way she could see the park was to look through a gap created by another seated couple. A tiny gap, because, being in love, they spent the majority of the time leaning in towards each other, scalps almost touching. When they pulled away to deposit a spoonful of food into their mouths or take little sips of wine, she took advantage of the viewing opportunity and greedily drank in a quick snapshot of the park.

Edith knew the restaurant would be expensive by the way the waiter shook out a cloth napkin onto her lap and filled the water glass to the brim. Even though Ricky had promised he would cover everything, she'd already paid for the hotel in advance and was worried about maxing out her credit card. She ordered a bowl of minestrone, hoping it would come with extra bread. The waiter withdrew from her quickly, and flitted around the other couple. Soon another waiter came over to their table with a bottle wrapped in a white cloth, and a flirtatious energy filled the room, oscillations of desire between the young couple and the two dark-eyed waiters, different permutations of body language and banter so that it was difficult to tell who was batting their thick lashes at whom.

The cynic in her questioned the performance, the waiters' motives. Truth be told, New York was all about the money—Edith had recognised that already. Throwing those dollar bills to waiters, taxi drivers, doormen, bellhops, when she should have been the one holding out her hand. Edith thought about her earlier life and whether she could have survived here on her own. A penniless, talentless girl. No, New York would have gobbled her up. Though there was always the groupie thing, attaching yourself to someone else's glitter and gold, before you end up barefoot and back in Nebraska.

\*\*\*

Edith hadn't spoken to Ricky in years, so when he had reached out to her via Facebook a month earlier, she was surprised. She'd had little contact with him since university and the unpleasantness of the graduation ceremony, and mainly kept up with all of his accomplishments through their common circle of friends. *Have you heard Ricky is doing a one-man show at Fringe? Have you seen Ricky in the new TV series on SBS?* It was better to hear it from others, for she couldn't continue to fake her enthusiasm over the phone; her voice gradually gave way to an insincerity—you could detect it in the lengthened vowels—*Oooooh, how wonderful!*—a widening arc of despair. It seemed that Ricky was the better actor after all.

They had first met during orientation week, signing up for Theatre Sports, and then sat in the same row during the first Semiotics of Performance lecture. Edith had recognised Ricky instantly by the purple happy pants and his erect dancer's posture—all the other students slouched back, into their chairs. From a distance he could have passed as Chinese—pale, angular face, short black hair and almond eyes—but only when Edith finally spoke to him at length did she get a chance to examine his face up close, and she was surprised to see he was wearing makeup: a thick paste to mask his acne, and eyeliner drawn up into cat's eyes.

Edith hadn't warmed to Ricky immediately. She was brought up in a long line of Methodists, and although her parents weren't particularly religious, 'the meek shall inherit the earth' sentiment had morphed over time into 'thou shalt not blow one's own trumpet'. Ricky was loud and brash, and promoted himself at every opportunity. He pushed himself into conversational clusters and friendship cliques, and if at first he was barely tolerated, over time, by way of default, he became a necessary fixture. For Ricky livened up every party, converted every small event into a grand occasion, and being around him made everyone feel more talented and special. Especially Edith. She developed a theatrical flair, swapped her khaki shorts and baggy T-shirts for black leggings and sparkly tops, and wore massive hooped earrings that pulled at her lobes. Soon it became the Ricky and Edith show: they began to act like a couple, sharing lifts to classes or having a private bitch in the refectory before the others turned up for drinks. But they weren't really a couple, were they? For even in those special alone times with Ricky, she sometimes sensed a restlessness in him, a need to search out something better in the room, while she yabbered on about the latest production dramas. There was also the matter of his sexuality. One night when they had been out dancing at a club they had come back to his student room and fallen exhausted onto his bed. She had drunkenly made a pass at him, but he pushed her off deftly, rolled her away like a spare piece of carpet. She recovered from the humiliation by reimagining

Ricky as gay, but when he showed no interest in any of the boys in their class either, Edith began to see him as hermaphroditic—self-loving, like a snail.

The Head of Performance, Horst Steinway, wasn't so enamoured with Ricky, and neither were the other tutors. Ricky lost out on all the plum roles to Edith and a serious-looking student called Fabian, who wore John Lennon glasses, a Che Guevara beret, and a black duffle coat even on forty-degree days. But nothing stopped Ricky's indefatigable, irrepressible star quality. When he was cast as a hatstand in the Dario Fo play *Trumpets and Raspberries* he outshone everyone by bursting forth from his prop and doing some odd Butoh thing with his mouth. He brought the house down. Afterwards, Edith's parents had spent more time raving about his performance than her own, which was as the lead. *Oooh, that Ricky, he's a scream*, her mum had said. *You can't keep your eyes off him.* The other cast members laughed it off, but Edith was rattled, and Fabian, who was incensed at being upstaged by *that little shit*, threatened to take Ricky outside and give him a right thrashing. Everyone knew it was pure bluster: Fabian's revolutionary capabilities were limited exclusively to his wardrobe.

And then, after university, when everyone else was applying for NIDA (some for the third time), Ricky did the unthinkable—he got himself an agent, moved to Sydney and started to make a name for himself on the stage and small screen, while Edith and the others drifted in and out of community theatre, and into sensible nine-to-five paying jobs. It was during a lunchtime break at the reception desk at the Sunset Retirement Village that Edith took the call from Ricky informing her that he had won the Green Card Lottery and was off to live in New York. He might as well have told her that he had just won a golden ticket to the rest of his life.

\* \* \*

Ricky was held up again in dress rehearsals, but he texted Edith to say they would finally meet for drinks in a small piano bar in the West Village. Marie's Crisis, originally a prostitutes' den in the 1850s, and now the go-to place for Broadway stars who came here on their days off to belt out show tunes. Or that's what Ricky had told Edith. But as she descended the stairs into the dingy, dark bar, she could see that the place was filled with predominantly gay men and tourists like herself, all hoping to experience something more than the balding man at the piano singing 'You're the Tops' in B flat. Before Edith could find Ricky, she was accosted by a pushy waitress, who demanded she order a drink or leave the premises. So Edith ordered a gin and tonic, handed over a ten-dollar bill, and then searched for Ricky's face in the packed room. It was difficult to see anything in the dim light. She concentrated on all the men on their own, but even then she couldn't be certain. The photo on Ricky's IMDb and Facebook profiles seemed to have been taken years ago, when Ricky was about thirty—unless he had also been lucky in the DNA stakes and simply looked fabulous for his age.

One of the men standing at the back smiled at her, so she gave a tentative wave and he nodded back. She made her way towards him, feeling her stomach churn over and do small flips as if she was a teenage girl again. Close up she could see that it wasn't Ricky, though in a perverse way, she would have been glad if it was. For the man's face was weirdly putty-like—plumped, yet at the same time stretched tight, like a dried animal skin over sharp cheekbones—and his hairline a block of filled-in colour, as if someone had spray-painted black around his temples. Edith knew that effect. She had gone to a new hairdresser in the mall the day before she flew out and was shocked, when she was led back to the mirror, to see the same muddy colour at her roots also staining her forehead. Her previous salt-and-pepper locks were now a uniform, dull brown, and as the young girl had stood talking to Edith (but really talking to her own reflection) she had cut Edith's hair in blunt, unflattering layers, so that Edith's head looked lopsided, and the beginnings of a double chin were more apparent. Edith looked terrible. The Japanese had a word for it. *Age-otori*. People who look worse after a haircut. Edith had seen the same thing with her parents' poodle, Tiffany, when she came back from the doggy groomer's. How as soon as the bouncy white curls were shorn away, the true nature of their pet was revealed: splotchy eczema-ravaged skin and a ratty head and tail—though it's funny how people can quickly forgive the ugliness of a dog.

'You're not Ricky?' she asked hopefully.

'Sammy,' he shouted back.

Edith stayed next to him for the rest of the evening, even when the text came through from Ricky saying that he was tied up and couldn't make it after all. When Sammy and a group of Finnish students dressed in red anoraks sang along to a rendition of 'Over the Rainbow', Edith joined in too. She could hear that Sammy's voice was rather good, far better than her own and that of the piano player, who was desperately trying to lob his voice an octave above the boisterous crowd. Edith looked around at all the people. Some were young and beautiful, with all the giddy expectancy of youth. Others, like Sammy, were deluded old fools. But here they all were, playing their part in this parallel universe to fame and fortune, as if better versions of themselves were out there already, treading the boards of Broadway, their names up in lights.

At eleven o'clock, Edith felt waves of nausea flow over her body and knew she couldn't stay awake any longer. She said goodbye to Sammy, and they embraced in that fake theatrical way, like she and Ricky used to do, giant smacks as if sealing lipstick on a tissue. One of Sammy's eyebrows had smeared off, winging its way to join the dye in his hairline, and his face shone with a film of sweat so that he looked like a waxwork exhibit starting to soften.

'Have a fabulous life, gorgeous,' he said.

'You too, gorgeous.'

Edith walked up the stairs and back onto the street, into a fierce, biting wind. No matter which way she turned, it felt as if she was being stung by a million tiny whips. Other people moved past her quickly, their heads bowed down in homage to the pavement, knowing exactly where they needed to be; Edith didn't even know how to hail a taxi. She thought about Ricky, and what he might be doing at that precise moment. She could picture him standing in the wings during the dress rehearsal as he waited to time his entrance perfectly. One red dot painted in one corner of his eye, a white dot in the other, and thick black eyeliner adding to the whole eye-widening effect, so that he looked like a fearsome demigod—as terrifying as Kali—about to orchestrate more destruction on an unrepentant, undeserving world.

\* \* \*

When the text came through at 11:11, the first thing Edith thought of was Legs Eleven. A throwback to when she organised the bingo events at the retirement home. The second thing she thought was: What the hell are you playing at, Ricky?

For Ricky had once again cancelled on her. Alas, he couldn't meet for lunch, but could she meet him instead at 4pm at Laughing Man Coffee in the Tribeca neighbourhood?

There he would give her the dress circle tickets for his opening night show.

*I can't wait to finally see you E!*

Seeing 'E!' on the small phone screen disturbed Edith. It had been years since she'd abbreviated her name to that, and now it seemed so ridiculous to shout out such a thing to the world, a childish squeak that could easily be lost in the wind.

Edith searched the address on her map and worked out that it would take her about half an hour to walk the distance, taking into account her sore Achilles heel and her terrible sense of direction. She knew she was running out of money fast, and couldn't afford to catch a cab. Soon she would be drawing down on her mortgage account, going backwards in this game of life. Funnily enough her parents hadn't thought this trip was a wasteful extravagance. Edith believed her mother had wanted this more than her, to boast to her friends that Edith was actually going somewhere, *off to New York to visit her famous friend!*

When it was time to leave to meet Ricky, Edith held her breath, and made her way to the elevators. The long, dark corridor was under-lit by small floor lights, which gave off a wan red glow like a bordello on a budget. It might have been a ploy to make the hotel seem cool and edgy, though Edith suspected it was really a way to cut down on cleaning costs: if you can't see the dirt, it doesn't exist.

She felt once again that sense of déjà vu—though not exactly a *lived* memory—more like she was walking through her own dream sequence. And then she remembered what it was. Why, yes! All those times watching *Twin Peaks* with Ricky, once a week buying the doughnuts and then lying on his unmade bed in front of the small TV screen—in the days before Netflix and live streaming, when everything had to be timed and primed for an exact moment. She couldn't remember every detail of the show, even doubted whether there were hotels with dark, lonely corridors and dim lighting, but it was something more, wasn't it? An other-worldly glow flickering from the screen (beautiful actors, weirdly mashed narratives), Ricky *ooh-ahhing* about perfect cheekbones and lips, and the strangled light escaping from the bedside lamp, which Edith had smothered with a red-patterned scarf so that the colours bled through like the flesh of blood oranges. There were the two of them on the bed, stripped down to comfort, bare legs semi-entwined like crooked boughs on a tree—and that first taste of sugared doughnuts, so sweet and easy on the mouth, but then sticking heavily on the way down, a pebble in a gull's gullet, as you hear the words of your best friend, *Hey, what's that funky smell, Edith—is it your fanny or your feet?*

The elevator pinged open to reveal a group of guests inside, the kind of young people she had grown to expect at 11 Howard. And there were no children, something which she now realised was apparent about SoHo in general. No prams in the street, no harried mothers trying to schlep small children across busy crossings. Edith imagined that this part of New York City was too expensive for most families, who were forced to live in more affordable boroughs further out from the heart of the city.

She wondered what these people did for a living. They could be techies, because that was where the money was now, certainly not in aged care. One girl had boyish clothes and her hair hurriedly scraped in a messy ponytail. Then there was an Asian boy with burgundy red–framed glasses, and another guy with shaggy, blonde-tipped hair—the type of hair wasted on a man. And they all stood in silence, a shared understanding that breathing in recycled air in a confined space was intimacy enough.

They arrived in the lobby and Edith quickly walked out, pushing open the heavy front door herself before the doorman could do so, another way to save a buck. It was still cold; though the bitter wind from the previous evening had died away, the sky remained a dismal grey, just like the great chunks of ice dotted with dirt and scuffed to the sides of the kerb. Edith walked past storefronts, slick cafés, and cheap diners with breakfast specials. Dead Christmas trees had been dumped on the sidewalks, their uppermost fronds creeping with brown. There was a pop-up shop on a corner that she had already wandered through on the first day in New York: separate stalls within the one giant space, an eclectic mix of crafts and fashion and second-hand goods all run by people a generation younger than herself. Here she had bought a felt bowler hat with a leopard-skin bow, one which she wore now, even though she was too old for second-hand clothing. It just made her look like a bag lady, or worse, a sad clown with spools of wiry, coarse hair sticking out from her ears. *The texture of pubes*, the young hairdresser had informed her after dabbing extra brown dye along her hairline.

In one of the stalls Edith had also spied a pair of sparkly silver stilettos, and they reminded her of the shoes she'd bought for her graduation: red glitter shoes with killer heels, the sort that could pierce a heart. Both Edith and Ricky had planned their wardrobe, knowing that only the shoes would matter when the flotilla of black gowns and mortarboards sailed across the stage. But Ricky had bailed on her, didn't make the effort to attend something as boring and archaic as a ceremony, didn't even bother letting her know. And then, when the procession of shoes finally marched in front of the audience—mostly sensible courts and black lace-ups, except for Fabian's combat boots—when it was Edith's turn, clipping across in the shoes that didn't work without Ricky, she could have sworn that all her weight went bearing down into those two needle-sharp points, and that she would fall into the boards of the stage and disappear forever.

* * *

Closer to Tribeca, the pedestrians thinned out, and the buildings seemed to grow statelier and more historic. The streets looked cleaner too, with no dead, thrown-away Christmas trees, making Edith wonder if this was the Jewish end of town. She checked her destination on Google Maps and then scanned the street for any signs of the café. How odd. This should be the location of Laughing Man Coffee, but she couldn't work out where it was. She saw a couple walking past with a pram and decided to ask them.

'Sure. You're almost there,' the woman said, pointing across the street.

'Oh. Thanks.'

'Australian, right? You'll get your first decent coffee.'

Edith smiled. The family were obviously Australian too, though probably from the east coast, and knew how to dress for winter—impressive designer coats and scarves, and their infant child, a little pufferfish in a heavy-duty padded jacket and rosy apple-ball cheeks.

Edith thanked them and crossed the street. She saw two large women (Two Fat Ladies—88) sitting outside the café on upturned boxes sipping takeaway coffees, and another on the window sill of the next-door shop. Obviously the best place for coffee. But when Edith walked inside she was stunned to see that it wasn't a café at all, just a counter and two staff members working the espresso machines, shelves lined with merchandise and nowhere to sit, and a group of customers waiting in the small, cramped space for their orders. It didn't make sense that this was the chosen place for the momentous, long-awaited reunion.

And then Edith realised, with a stab of dismay, that Ricky hadn't intended staying to chat: it was merely the spot for the exchange of theatre tickets, as hurried as a drug deal drop.

Edith looked at the sign on the wall, a message of hope and altruism from the owner, Broadway and screen legend Hugh Jackman. She glanced at her watch, which showed that Ricky was already two minutes late. 58—Make Them Wait. Thought properly, for the first time, about how weird it was that she could never find out a thing about Ricky's play on the Internet and how the timeline of Ricky's successes had abruptly stopped eighteen years ago.

And then she heard the heralding sound of a new text coming in and she didn't need to read it to guess what it would say. 62—Turn the Screw. For Edith knew, suddenly, and with a cold, sharp clarity, that she and Ricky would never meet. She doubted that he was even in New York— was probably back in the brick and asbestos-lined suburbs of Perth, laughing while he played this cruel game with her.

But she deserved it, didn't she? For she had played her own wicked hand on Ricky: a series of terrible betrayals over the years. First, sleeping with Fabian straight after that awful graduation night, trying not to flinch when she saw the pale, scrawny self he revealed as he stripped off the gown, the coat, the boots, the beret, the glasses. And each time she met up with Fabian after that evening, it wasn't just the ritual of coarse, jabbing sex, but their shared loathing of Ricky, becoming uglier and uglier in their comments and observations; and then in the later years taking this bitchiness online and infecting the other class members in the group chats with their mean spiritedness. But it was never ever satisfying for Edith. Not really. For after the first flush of guilty pleasure, she was left only with the nasty aftertaste of bile.

Edith ordered a flat white and waited with the other customers. She thought about all the conversations with Ricky about acting. How method acting only worked if you said yes to everything—too many noes closing down the scene. And that the whole point of Liza Minnelli in *Cabaret* was to play a performer who could never really cut it on the stage. *See Edith, what people don't get is that Liza was never that good. She was only good at playing someone who was terrible... a mediocre B-grade performer.* Edith could see now that in the dying years of Liza's career, the only method acting she could summon up was tremulous befuddlement, essentially becoming her sad, old self.

When Edith's name was called out she stepped forward for her coffee ('Edie' was scribbled on the cup), then she went outside and walked along the streets until she found a beautiful classic brownstone with wide, welcoming steps. She tucked the wiry coils of hair behind her ears, adjusted the hat and tilted her head back, placing her tongue at the roof of her mouth, something which Ricky had taught her as a way to create a better jawline. She took a selfie to photoshop and post later on Facebook with the caption: *Staying in New York with the ever-fabulous Ricky. What a legend!*

# BEES OF PARIS

From the rooftop there was little symmetry, unlike the grand Parisian avenues with their mesmerising alignment of chestnut and linden trees. No, from here Louise could see where each apartment abutted and jutted into the other; all the illegal add-ons, the cracked, peeling angles, the dodgy workmanship—the fire traps that would never be allowed in Australia. She didn't know what was more disappointing, the view from the small terrace or the rented room itself, which was no bigger than a modest laundry back home.

As Louise stood there contemplating the bleak scene, and trying to imagine living a Thumbelina-like existence for the next month, a flicker of movement in her peripheral vision made her turn. There on the adjacent apartment roof was a white-suited figure, dressed like an astronaut and wildly waving. Louise started to wave back then realised her mistake. The person wasn't being friendly but flapping in panic at dark specks that dotted the clear blue sky. *Bees.* Louise watched with interest, for she understood what it was like, that first moment when you remove the top honey frame—the supers—and the assault begins.

The beekeeper continued to flap and gesticulate, hopping from one leg to the other, smoker puffing aimlessly skyward—seemingly losing the battle—and then without a sound, the person dropped like a stone over the steep ledge.

Louise felt an ache in her groin, that place where the fear always took hold, and screamed.

She ran inside and grabbed her mobile, trying to remember what the emergency number in France was. Surely not 911? She abandoned the call and ran down the flights of steps, leaping three at a time, surprising the concierge at the desk.

'Someone's fallen off the roof,' she managed to pant out.

'Pardon?' The old man seemed unable to comprehend her urgency.

'Someone's fallen next door. Can you call an ambulance?'

He spoke so fast in French that she felt like he was spitting at her, and for the first time she understood what it was like to be excluded from another culture.

'Forget it,' Louise shouted as she ran outside, looking up at the building to get her bearings, to work out where her room was located.

She darted around the side street, recognised the blue doorway with the colourful planter boxes she had seen earlier from her balcony, and knew the other building must be that grey stone one to her left. She sprinted down the back alley, but there was no body lying on the ground, no-one wailing over a loved one. Had she simply imagined everything? She walked back to the front of the building, beginning to doubt her spatial awareness, when a woman dressed in lime and black lycra and wheeling a bicycle came out through the front door.

'Do you speak English?' Louise asked her.

'A little.'

'I think someone fell off your roof.'

'Who fell?'

'I don't know. Is someone keeping bees up there?'

'You mean the American?'

'I think so. Yes. Can I... How do I get to the roof?'

'So you're here about the bees?'

'Yes,' Louise lied.

'Okay, you can go in.' The woman rang the bell and a man's voice came through low and seductive on the intercom and then Louise was buzzed in.

The interior reminded her of her grandmother's nursing home: threadbare carpet, and an abrasive smell of disinfectant that seemed only to worsen the odour it was trying to mask. She travelled through the corridor, passing the different rooms, reading the names on placards—Clairaut, Roux, Durand—and then upstairs, climbing three creaking flights until she came to the very top landing. Here there was only one room: 'Ms Evelyn Parks'. She knocked on the door but there was no reply, and when she tried the handle it remained fast. Then she spied the hatch window in the far corner, opening out onto a large sill about a metre above the roofline. She climbed through, jumped down, and saw the wooden bee boxes stacked high like a filing cabinet, and the abandoned frame of honeycomb, which the bees had settled back on to, a bubbling mass of amber and brown bodies.

'Hello, can you help me?'

Surprised, Louise turned to see that what she thought was a steep drop to the streets below was in fact another parapet set lower down, and there the beekeeper was sitting, leg stretched out in front.

'I think I've sprained my ankle.' The voice was a woman's and the twang clearly American.

'I'll come to you.'

Louise sat on the edge and then let her body drop down, feeling the ground shudder through her shins.

'Let me see your ankle.'

It was obviously swollen, the blue and purple discolouration already surfacing through the doughy white flesh.

'Are you a nurse?'

'No,' Louise replied, and sensed the woman's disappointment.

'It was the bees. They were too angry.'

'You really need two people to work the boxes. One to remove the supers, the other to quieten them with the smoker.'

'You know about bees?'

'A little. I used to date someone who was...' she paused for the right words, '... into bees.'

'How wonderful!' The woman removed her round bee hat, and a couple of dead bees fell to the ground. Louise was startled at this sudden revealing of her head; she wasn't prepared for such a large fleshy face, for overripe lips and grey-blonde hair cut like a man's.

'You must stay and help me with the bees. I'm a novice.'

'I'm only here for a month, then I'm off to Italy.'

'Where are you staying?'

'La Roxy.'

'Terrible place. Full of whores. No, you can help me here, stay free of charge.'

Louise wanted to protest but there was something compelling about this woman. Maybe it was the accent that weighted every utterance with a sense of purpose, or the way she sat there motionless, face tilted upwards as if ripening further in the French sun. Really, Louise had no choice. It was a fait accompli.

\* \* \*

Evelyn Parks had been an English Major at Stanford University, worked as an intern at Little, Brown and then stayed on for years in the editorial department, until one day at the age of thirty-nine (same age as Louise!) packed it all in (the rent-controlled apartment on the Lower East Side, the inherited cat) and left for Europe.

'I wanted to *live* the book, not write it,' she told Louise that first night over a supper of warm lentil salad and stale baguette. 'And, I am doing just that.' She took a breath in between bites. 'Of course, this district has changed a lot since I've been here. The markets have become more touristy, the best *boulangerie* closed down, and ever since that damn Australian journalist wrote that book about Rue Montorgueil, it's been crawling with Australians.'

Louise wasn't sure if she was meant to laugh at this or feign offence. She settled for a weak smile.

'But tourists are good for the honey market,' the woman continued. 'A little jar of authentic Parisian honey to take as gifts for the folks back home.'

'Can you make much money?'

'Hell, yes. I'm told bees can produce sixty kilos of honey a hive. At fifteen dollars a jar that's a tidy sum. At least it will keep the dream alive.'

By all accounts it looked like Evelyn was only barely doing that. The apartment was in desperate need of a refurbishment, she kept only one light bulb burning at any given time—tonight it was the pendant light hanging over the little table in the kitchen—and five years ago she'd had to partition off half her flat to rent out to a tenant. Louise couldn't quite determine where the tenant entered the apartment (there was only one door on this floor), but at night as she lay in her lumpy camp bed, she could hear someone moving around on the other side of her wall, as if permanently entombed.

The next morning they immediately started working with the bees. Evelyn was in charge of the smoker but sat on a stool to rest her ankle, while Louise set to work removing the frames. She was wearing the bee suit (Evelyn wore long-sleeved overalls) and she moved quickly, prising each frame apart, brushing the bees away with the horsehair brush and then bagging each frame in plastic. The hive was in a shocking condition. The brood had got into the supers box, and it was a mess, with some of the comb gnawed and almost black from the larva faeces and cocoons. Louise guessed Evelyn was the type who didn't believe in using a queen excluder. God, she thought she had forgotten all of that. It was funny how much she still remembered after four years. *Bees don't like dark blue.* She had been wearing a dark blue suit the first day they'd met—her work suit—and he stood arms folded, an unbending man, making her feel like a small child. She had been flirty on the phone, normally good at cajoling and convincing people to be interviewed for the local paper, but then, standing in front of him, she had lost all her power.

*Do you want me to change into something else*, she had replied, but it came out dirty and wrong. She couldn't tell if it was amusement that played on his mouth or disapproval. *A quiet queen calms the hive*, he'd said in his measured voice. Louise nodded and also wrote that down in her notebook, under the heading 'Bee-Keeping Fast Facts', then, doubting his sincerity, glanced up to see him smiling at her. A relationship that lasted only three months and two days, and still she remembered it all. He was her last boyfriend—there was little opportunity to meet men at a workplace filled mainly with women—and she was to unfortunately discover you are only ever defined by your most recent relationship.

But she had to focus on the job at hand. The lavender smoke wasn't calming Evelyn's angry bees. She felt them hitting against her suit like a small army and wondered if they were Africanised (another thing she remembered). She decided to only remove three frames at a time, since Evelyn didn't have an extractor and harvesting honey manually was an arduous task, best carried out over days. Louise heaved each bagged-up frame back to the apartment and, with Evelyn encouraging her from her chair, started to extract honey from the comb, first slicing the waxy caps off, like scales, then pressing slabs of comb through a sieve and letting the honey ooze out. With so much debris in the honey, she had to re-sieve it using a stocking, before pouring the thick liquid into the settling bucket. The honey was so dark, so unappealing, and she wondered if Evelyn knew that lighter honey commanded a much higher price.

Suddenly, it occurred to Louise that she hadn't seen the queen for some time, that she hadn't taken care to look for her. In her own haste, she wouldn't have noticed if the queen had crawled to the top frame and then been inadvertently brushed away, onto the ground.

'Evelyn, you have to get a queen excluder. It will keep her in the brood box, stop her from moving to the next level and laying eggs all through the honeycomb.'

'Rubbish, I want my queen to have free reign of the hive. I don't want to hem her in.'

'But the honey is so dark,' Louise ventured.

'I'll market it as tulip and poplar honey. That's known to be darker in colour. As long as it's Parisian no-one will care.'

Evelyn, wedged into her armchair with a pile of weighty books, looked like she wouldn't budge on anything.

\* \* \*

It took a few days for the honey to settle and the impurities to finally float to the top. After that Louise bottled non-stop: sterilising, pouring and pasting home-made labels—'Authentic Parisian Honey'—onto each jar. Evelyn (still with one eye on her book) supervised everything from her armchair. Louise's throat burned from the constant sampling. Not that she liked honey, but each time some dripped over the side of the glass jar, she wiped it away with her finger, sucking it off and questioning the strangeness of its musky aftertaste. Everything affected the taste of honey: the way it was processed, the type of flowers. *That* was something else she remembered.

The weekend after the interview, she'd accompanied him on the long drive to check his hives, scattered across the South West, and strategically positioned to follow the jarrah blooms. After kilometres of muted grey bush, she exclaimed loudly when it transformed into fields of vivid yellow. *Canola has a higher glucose level*, he remarked. *Lacks the smooth floral notes of jarrah.* She didn't write that down; she knew she was being judged. When they arrived at his hives set back in the bush, all she could see was the stack of drab boxes in the distance and the bees buzzing around them as if they were circling a decomposing body.

Louise couldn't fault their sexual compatibility. When they finally slept together at his house, their bodies matched perfectly in a quiet, satisfying rhythm, so that it felt as if she had arrived home. Patterns in leaves, the symmetry of ant trails, puffs of pale blossoms on paperbarks, a joyous chorus of birdsong that burst across a city skyline... all were guiding her as lights do on a runway... to him, to them, to a foreseeable future of children—their little faces peering out from secret hideaways in trees. Everything seemed so right, and yet Louise couldn't explain that feeling of suffocation whenever he cupped her face to kiss her.

Years later, whenever she felt the despair of being alone, of leaving a man for no real reason, it was that image she clung to: the struggle to catch her breath while they kissed. And also the memory of him marking his newly acquired queen with an orange dot, holding her down firmly under the fluorescent light while he inked her small abdomen.

\* \* \*

If Louise felt any resentment about the time she was wasting on the honey, her outrage only deepened when Evelyn suggested that she should also be the one to do the selling.

'But I can't speak French,' she protested.

'All you have to do is be charming,' said Evelyn, her large face expanding into a Southern belle grin.

So Louise found herself dressed up, at Evelyn's suggestion, in a tight skirt and high heels and lugging one of the cartons down to the market street. But as she wobbled along the cobbled streets she felt uncomfortable; so gawky and large—like those tall girls in the primary school photos, the netballers who matured too early.

At the first couple of shops, she was rudely waved away before she even had a chance to deliver her rehearsed spiel. The next grocer took one look at her honey, showed her a stack of his own on the shelves and shrugged. There was no need for words. Everywhere she went there was plenty of honey, all lightly coloured, with hand-drawn labels beautifully sketched and etched in black ink. *The Bees of Paris*, one *pâttisier* explained to her as she admired the cabinet full of glistening chocolate bees, which oozed centres of honey when bitten. From the rooftops of the Opéra national de Paris and swank city hotels, to the small terrace home gardens—everyone it seemed was keeping bees. Louise was told that due to the widespread use of pesticides, bee populations in the countryside had dwindled to dangerously low numbers. But here in the city, the bees of Paris were thriving, lilting from cherry blossom to chestnut blossom and across all the window boxes, gardens and trees of the spiralling twelve *arrondissements*. A beautiful tale of survival at all odds—but not for poor Evelyn, who had failed to see what was happening outside her own front door.

Louise had had enough. Her back was aching from wearing heels, and she needed to constantly set down the box to rest her arms. She decided to take the metro back to the apartment. Evelyn had given her instructions to get out at Strasbourg–Saint-Denis and walk up the second *rue*, to the left of the arch. However, as Louise struggled up the staircase from the platform she realised there was more than one exit. Emerging from the metro she saw two arches, made a wild guess and immediately found herself in a street that had a different vibe to the area she was staying in, more downbeat, and seedier. She averted her eyes from a shop selling porn DVDs and a prostitute 'giving it a go' in daylight. She hugged her box as she passed shop fronts selling garments, which even in a culture she didn't understand stood out as cheap and tacky. As she forced herself to keep going, a dark-skinned man dressed like a pimp sauntered towards her with arms outstretched and a mock smile on his face. And Louise knew he was taking the piss out of her, that at her age and in her clumsy shoes she could never be one of his girls. She wanted to shout at him, but instead did the only thing that women in this situation could do: pursed her lips and deliberately blanked him. By the time she found her way back to Evelyn's apartment, the carton had weakened and split so much that she had to abandon all the jars in the nearby alleyway.

As she was climbing the stairs, she bumped into the cyclist she'd met the previous week.

'What's happening with the bees?' the woman demanded.

'What do you mean?'

'They are swarming and stinging the children. Where are your permits?'

'I'll speak to Evelyn.'

'She shouldn't be keeping bees,' she hissed. Louise nodded, and quickly made her escape.

Evelyn greeted her at the door with a kiss.

'How did you go?'

'Great. All gone,' Louise said, taking out the money she'd been refunded from La Roxy and placing it on the kitchen table.

'I knew it!' Evelyn did a victory hop around the room, and then sank down onto a chair, exhausted.

Louise smiled, then excused herself to pack. Tomorrow, she would leave Paris behind, take the first train out to the French countryside and follow the fields of furrowed gold. On a whim, she knocked on the wall behind her bed, and gave a laugh when she heard the three knocks sound in reply.

# IN TRANSIT

Everything about my mother's side of the family is half-arsed. Uncle Maurie's unfinished carport extension, my grandfather who stops shaving at his chin so that his neck looks like a white woolly llama's, and the way my mother tries to kill herself. This time, the half-emptied bottle of diazepam on the bedside table and my plastic Tinker Bell tumbler next to it, Tink's face disintegrating and blurry from too many dishwasher cycles. It's easier to focus on that cup than Mum, who lies on the gurney with an oxygen mask cupped over her mouth and her cheeks slackened pouches, falling gracelessly to one side.

The paramedics allow me to sit in the front cab, and we race down the hill that leads to the main highway and then a twenty-minute drive to the new Perth hospital. The woman driving the ambulance is probably the same age as my mum. She has a tightly coiled energy; you can see it in the hands that grip the steering wheel and her army-style efficiency when changing lanes. Maybe she unravels at night with a bottle of wine after her shift has finished, but for now it's all focus and restrained chit-chat. She fires questions at me: what year am I in at school, what will I study next year, and has my mum done this before. I give the standard answers, I know the routine, and she gives a cursory nod, a sympathetic sound through her clamped teeth because she knows how much of herself she needs to reveal too. She is all professional on the radio, follows standard procedures as I stare out the window and pretend to be watching the traffic. What I am really doing is jumping over stuff. Anything: lamp posts, street signs, bus stops. In my mind's eye I am running along the edge of the road and then I hurdle over things, and sometimes my stride is even and the jumps are well paced, and then other times there are too many things to go over and I start to stumble and lose control. I hate this feeling and try to run faster, lift my legs higher, but the rhythm is all wrong and I end up feeling out of kilter. I want to stop but I can't.

We slow down at a set of traffic lights where drivers seem confused as to what to do. One lady attempts to swing her wheels onto the middle island to let us pass but there is not enough room, and I can see the flustered panic as she twists and strains to see her other options. This is the same set of traffic lights where Mum and I stopped on the way back from the drama showcase night at the beginning of the year. There wasn't much traffic around, just two other cars in front of us waiting for the signal to turn green. Suddenly, two guys got out of their cars and started to dance in opposite directions, doing a slow, lilting jig around their vehicles, smiling like quixotic Irish pixies lost in their own private joke. Mum's instinct was to press her locking device, begin to say *druggies*. But then she started to get the giggles, tiny tremors of happiness rocking her shoulders, and I couldn't help but join in. So there were the two of us laughing; the car gently shaking, and us locked into this world of mild hysteria together.

I know it's not appropriate to tell the paramedic this—she is too focused on getting the ambulance through the lights and past the minefield of after-school traffic—but I want to tell her that in drama class we have been studying the light and shades of a dramatic arc, and how in every play there is a moment of lightness, a certain levity that gives relief to the tragedy to come. A wedding waltz, a bawdy song, a country dance. And now as I watch the woman in front of us half stranded on her concrete island, with nowhere to go, I am frightened that Mum has used up her one and only jig.

\* \* \*

The overweight male orderly leads me to the temporary locker room, which is really a cleaning storeroom. He apologises in a way that makes me think he has said it many times before. *A new hospital, teething problems, an issue with burst pipes*. He has a cheery cynicism that comes from working in mental health. I put my backpack in the locker, pocket the key, then follow him down the corridor where we are buzzed into another waiting room. Everything is new and shiny, and the art on the walls is too literal—a vase of flowers, a pastel seascape—with nothing abstract or religious, or likely to set off a new psychosis. I am not allowed to go into Mum's room but must wait for her to come to me. I can see through the large glass window a private courtyard with a newly planted garden of natives, but I know the rules. It's too dangerous for her to be anywhere but in her small room, drugged up and highly supervised.

Before Mum comes out, a young guy with a clipboard clicks opens the door. He is dressed as if going to a university lecture, and I am startled to hear a strong Dutch accent, which makes him sound like a backpacker. Is he really a psychiatrist? He asks, how old am I, where is my father, has my mother done this before, and I explain everything to him, weighing up the pros and cons of each answer, not worried about him reading too much into anything. His training is fixated on medications, not the art of body language. So, he asks me again, is there no-one else at home, no adult to care for Mum over the next forty-eight hours, and I say, no. He thinks it is an unsatisfactory outcome; I am secretly relieved.

As soon as I see Mum shuffle across the room, I know that she has been told she has to stay locked up. She slumps into the vinyl chair next to the coffee table, her head bowed low and hair forming a greasy barrier over her face. I wait for the apology, but I get nothing. Instead she is breathing thinly, as if through a narrow straw.

And then a raspy plea. 'Can you ring Dad? You know I can't stay here.'

'No, I am not ringing Dad. Dad isn't an option.'

We sit in silence. I have nothing to say to her. The minutes drag by, and I can only imagine that if this was a test, if the hospital staff working on the other side of the glass partition were watching this scene play out, their pens would be frantically scribbling observations like 'hard-faced bitch of a daughter', 'as cold as ice'.

There's no point in staying so I leave, and I end up walking along the main road where there are patches of the original bushland in the grey, lifeless soil. I look for the Christmas trees but it's too early for the display of gaudy orange flowers. Last year Mum was obsessed with these trees. It made her happy to spot them on the side of the road and in pockets of bushland, or dotted around playgrounds in the suburbs. We even joined a treasure hunt put on by the Wildflower Society to find the Christmas trees in the bush with the special tags. Mum said she liked the idea of a prize. An elderly woman wearing Bermuda shorts walked beside us, explaining that *Nuytsia floribunda* was a type of native mistletoe, a semi-parasite that sends its roots out to sucker onto another plant's source of nutrients. I could tell that Mum was disappointed in hearing the word 'parasite', but she lightened up when she heard how the Noongar people believed that the spirits of the dead passed through these trees. *Like a transit lounge to a better place*, said Mum. And now looking back at the hospital, which dominates the sky like a small city, I wonder how many spirits are slipping out of stiff white corpses and winging their way to the branches of this tree, waiting for the final flare of iridescent colour.

And then my phone rings and it is the psychiatrist telling me in his strange clipped vowels that Mum's friend Derrick is signing her out.

\* \* \*

The hair comes off in one hit. Mum plaited it down her back like a horse's tail prepared for dressage to make it easier for the hairdresser at the mall to cut, and now it is swaddled in tissue paper. She hands it to me and I am worried that she wants me to store it as a keepsake in my undies drawer. The transformation is immediate. Her face looks less dragged down and tired; she doesn't look like a crazy old cat-hoarder any more. A whirlwind of life-force instantly rushes to her brain, like when you prune rose hips off a bush. It's as if all her energy was being sapped by that long lank hair. Once home, she can't stop cleaning, she can't stop baking. Each day when I return home from school there is the next batch of scones cooling off under a tea towel on the sink. She is obsessed with their height and researches on the Internet how to get more rise factor from each batch. *Don't overwork the dough, baste with milk, only twist once using a metal cutter.* How can I tell her I don't care if they're flat and disappointing—I am sick of the aftertaste of baking soda and crave vegetables for dinner. And then it is a week of pikelets, either gooey in the middle or burnt on the outside. Maybe I want the other version of Mum back, the one still in her terry towelling dressing-gown at three o'clock in the afternoon, flicking through the shopping channels.

Derrick doesn't seem to mind. He eats whatever is put in front of him, bits of crumb and cream flecking his already greying beard. Mum met him during her first stint in hospital, and they bonded over their mutual dislike of Lyn, the night nurse from hell. Derrick is a big man who moves about restlessly on our small kitchen chairs, forever trying to work out what to do with his legs. He seems like any normal guy except there is something weird about his forehead—a massive indent as if someone has spent a lifetime pressing a thumb into the bony ridge between his eyebrows. Mum and Derrick spread out their wellness recovery action plans across the kitchen table, taking up all the space with the pieces of paper and their elbows. It keeps them energised—that plus pots of stewed black tea, and the jargon that they like to use, which makes them sound like jaunty health professionals. Mum's latest expression is 'disorderly eating'—as opposed to eating disorder—and she repeats the different permutations as if the very order of the words gives more meaning to her life. She writes down her daily goals and long-term goals, but I notice on her Pinterest account she has posted them as her bucket list: *Swim with the whale sharks at Ningaloo*, *See Cirque du Soleil*, *Finish redecorating the spare room*, *Walk the Bibbulmun Track*, *Read War and Peace*, *Make a ceramic birdbath*. I see she has fifteen followers and knowing that Derrick is her only friend, how everyone else in her life has slowly dropped away, I wonder how many are random women from the American Midwest unaware they are liking the erratic wish list of a crazy lady on the other side of the world.

I don't see what Derrick has written. He is circumspect and private, and cups his hands around his bits of paper. All I know about him is that without the medication he hears three different voices, one telling him to write his manifesto, and the other two, nasty bullies constantly putting him down. I also know that when he was ten years old he was molested by a family friend, and refers to paedophiles as kiddie fiddlers, and it is this expression, the way it sounds more like children's party entertainers, that disturbs me more than my mother's bucket list.

\* \* \*

We drive through the treeless valley of shops with their sun-peeled signs and crumbling bitumen driveways, past the Toys "R" Us, Cash Converters and then the vacant shops with the For Lease signs taped across acres of dark glass. Mystical

Rainbows, says an old shop front, and I wonder who named it and who owned it and whether they sold shimmering useless things that broke in a strong wind.

Mum and I are off to Carousel to buy some black leggings for my final drama performance, and *to check out the sales*, says Mum, but it's easy to tell she is only half committed to this outing. She looks washed out, and there are dark smudges under her eyes as if she hasn't removed her eye makeup for over a week. I know she is having trouble sleeping at night. I hear her muffled sobs at two o'clock in the morning through my bedroom door and the thin whistle of the kettle letting out a nervous here-we-go-again sigh.

When we arrive the car park is full, and it takes Mum three circuits of the shopping centre to finally find a parking bay. As soon as we enter the food hall, the fried smells hit me hard and I realise how ravenous I really am. I want to ask Mum to stop for lunch but know that it is better to keep her moving, so we walk around the packed, chattering tables, and past the central pop-up shops. A young, pushy guy is spruiking organic moisturiser samples. He has the acumen of a car salesperson, and one quick glance at Mum makes him hesitate, wait instead for the woman walking directly behind us. As we pass each store, see the children still dressed in their Saturday sports gear, and the mothers all hassled and yelling at Dylans and Jordans to hurry up, it dawns on me that we have made a grave error in shopping on the Saturday before Father's Day.

'Let's try in here, Mum,' I say, pulling her into the relative safety of Lorna Jane.

I flick through the sales items, knowing they're still beyond our price range, and Mum stands at the entrance, hugging her handbag to her chest and blankly staring at the posters of beautiful women dressed in lycra. I take a pair of bike shorts off the rack, not really wanting them but doing anything to keep the momentum going. I leave Mum standing there while I quickly try them on, not caring if they are any good, just turning around in circles and different angles to check out my butt. I see the curtain rustle a little to the side and expect it to be Mum, but instead it is the shop assistant saying, 'I think there's something wrong with your mother.'

My heart does a nervous leap and I feel the sensation rise to my throat like vomit as I race out, and there is Mum talking with the other assistant, a tall blonde girl who bends like a primary school teacher to meet her face to face. And Mum is trying to communicate something, but her jaw is stalling and seizing like it has a faulty hinge, not able to release the caged words with the right timing. And I can see how the girl is transfixed by my mum's mouth, watching with a kind of fascination and then horror as she sees the tongue agitate and bob like a cocky's. Seeing something bluish-black and truncated, as if God or evolutionary forces have played a heartless trick on her.

IN TRANSIT

\* \* \*

My mobile rings and I recognise the number as being Dad's sister, Aunty Helen, so out of respect for Mum I take the call in the garden. I can picture Aunty Helen sitting on the French wicker stools at her polished marble kitchen counter, brushing away some imaginary crumbs, her back annoyingly erect like a Pilates instructor's. Her voice hurts my ear when she tells me that I need to leave immediately and go stay with Dad.

'Not yet,' I say, explaining that it is too close to my final exams and how the move will complicate things.

I wonder how much she really knows, and if anyone has told her that Mum hasn't left the house in days and that Derrick has checked himself into hospital again. The conversation looks like it will go on forever, stuck in the same old loop, so I find a sunny spot on the ground and lie down with the long blades of grass scratching at my bare legs. From this angle I can see across to the neglected garden beds, and the weeds sending up their tapered yellow heads. Or is it the *Nuytsia floribunda*? So I get up to take a closer look at the small sapling we planted last year, but it is flowerless; the plant looks barely alive. We never won the Christmas tree treasure hunt, but afterwards the old lady in the Bermuda shorts came looking for us, held out one of the potted prizes as a gift.

*Here*, she said, smiling mainly at me. *They are tricky to keep alive, but if they can latch onto the right plant—get the nutrients they need, well, you never know...*

And I thanked her, because I guess that is the polite thing to do.

# THE EGG

Even in his sleep, Bryant knew there was something wrong. The children's voices were more pitchy than usual, and where before he could allow a certain amount of light and noise to pulse in and out of his shallow dream life, now it had penetrated too deeply. Shit. He pulled on his jeans, which still held the loose, slack shape from when he had worn them hours earlier, and went looking for his eldest son.

'Casey, what's going on?' The boy was in the lounge room with his younger brother and the neighbour's kid who drifted in and out of their driveway, but whose name he never bothered to learn.

'Dad.'

There was no need for Casey to say anything else. There in the middle of the room stood an enormous egg.

'What the...'

'We found it in the dunes.'

'And we're keeping it,' added his youngest son, Ben, who laid his hand on the top of the egg as if he had just scaled its giddy heights.

'It's a dinosaur egg.' It was the first time Bryant had ever heard the neighbour's kid speak, and his voice sounded high and nasal.

'What the hell.' Bryant bent down to examine the specimen closer, and saw that, although ovoid in shape, its outer casing was hard and grainy in appearance, making it look more like a World War II relic. Ben tapped the surface with a fingernail.

'Get away from it!' Bryant didn't mean to yell, but he had visions of his wife coming home from work to a house smouldering in ash. If it was a bomb, it would need to be defused or removed with care.

'Dad, it's fine. We carried it from the dunes, didn't we?' Casey patted the egg. 'We love it and we're keeping it.'

Casey was probably right but that didn't stop Bryant from lightly pressing his ear against the egg to listen for a series of faint ticks.

'Is it going to hatch?' cried his youngest. 'Is it alive, Dad?' But all Bryant could hear were the children's shallow breaths and the dull thrum of his own ear against the egg's cool surface.

'Let's get it into the garage. We'll work out what it is later.'

Bryant carried the egg outside, and placed it carefully in the corner of the garage. He didn't know quite why, but he fetched a large white sheet from the laundry cupboard and draped it over the egg. Then he went back inside the house to try and get some more shut-eye, banning the children from going anywhere near the garage.

It was impossible to sleep. He lay on the bed, listening to the muffled sounds of excitement and, in the distance, a mower neatening a plot of green. And every time he changed position in the bed, he could smell the unwashed sheets and the stink of his armpits. He knew he wouldn't sleep. Soon his wife would be home, and there would be the clatter of pans, the cutlery drawer opening and closing, the sizzle and spit of oil and then a stir-fry would appear moments before he had to hop into his car for the forty-five-minute drive to the airport. A long drive where he could make plans, pay bills in his head and give a bit more consideration to things like that egg.

\* \* \*

Night shift at Perth Airport seemed to consist of two states of being. First, there was the hit-the-road-running part, where flights would arrive back to back, the arrivals hall would swell with a line of weary, rumpled travellers snaking all the way back to the escalators, and you only had forty seconds to process and stamp each passport. And then there was the hanging-around 'doing time' part in between flights, where the officers would lounge in their bunker, kick back on the lumpy couches and rummage for food in their bags, or grab salty snacks from the vending machine.

In a strange way Bryant preferred the busier part of the evening. The world would whirr past him in a flash of humanity, where the woollen coats and wrapped scarves of Europe would seamlessly morph into the bare midriffs and beaded braids of Bali. Forty seconds to eye a person and make a secret judgement about whether they should be coded on their declaration form for a baggage exam. Over twenty years of doing the job, Bryant had developed a sixth sense for what kind of traveller stood in front of him. He knew the type who would stash an extra bottle of Jim Beam in their hand luggage or the ones who would try to bring back a heritage tomato cutting from Italy. Of course, anyone transiting Colombia got put in for a full search. His eyes would flick from passport to face, to screen, back to face, all the while assessing the risk and keeping that neutral, easygoing smile fixed on his face. Lately, though, he'd found himself assessing people in a different kind of way. Those families, the families of four who were returning from a holiday at the theme parks in Florida or Euro Disney, the Dads whose stated occupation was 'electrician' and the mums who were nurses; staring at these families who could afford such a holiday, and there he was, a shift worker with a wife who also worked, barely meeting the mortgage repayments for his median-priced home in a suburb south of Perth. He didn't think he was jealous, just perplexed in the same way he was when he watched the younger colleagues at work being streamed ahead of himself into cushy promotions in Fremantle.

After the midnight and early morning flights had been processed, he found himself as usual walking back up to the recreation room with Eddie, another older officer who had trained in his year intake. The class of ACO 20: the last group to enter Customs through the regular public service exams, without needing a degree to get ahead.

'You look tired, mate.'

'I didn't get much sleep. The kids woke me all excited. They found a giant egg in the dunes.'

'An egg?'

'They think it's prehistoric.'

'Sounds like an elephant bird.'

'What?'

'Elephant bird. Remember the one found by a kid in Cervantes years ago? His family tried to auction it privately but the government stopped the sale because it was found on Crown land. The boy hid the egg, reburied it—only coughed it up once the State Government agreed to pay.'

Bryant vaguely remembered the story. An image of a boy and his dad on the news looking like they had just hit the jackpot.

'Be careful. It might be worth a fortune. Tell them you found it in your backyard.'

'I'm sure it's nothing,' grinned Bryant, but something like hope fluttered in his heart and stayed with him all shift.

\*\*\*

That afternoon, once he had slept and showered, Bryant set to work researching the egg. He found out that the kid in Cervantes got an ex gratia payment of $25,000 from the State Government but on the open market it could have fetched five times that amount. He also discovered that the watermelon-sized egg had drifted from Madagascan shores and somehow found its way across the Indian Ocean to Western Australia to lie dormant in the sand for thousands of years. The trouble was, their egg was bigger than that of the extinct elephant bird. He found another site that talked about giant prehistoric emus, but there were no pictures to verify what they had in their garage. Every now and then he questioned if it really was an egg at all, and he'd lift the roller door to go peer under the sheet, and trace his fingers over the rough, dark coating.

Bryant took a photo of the egg from different angles, a few close-ups, and one with a chicken egg placed beside it to provide a sense of scale and then attached these to an email addressed to the Head of Palaeontology at the city museum. He kept the story short and to the point, being careful not to give away any personal details. His reasoning was simple: in order to sell the egg privately he needed to know exactly what it was. He was surprised when a reply bounced back at him within minutes.

*Dear Sir/Madam,*

*I am very interested in examining your specimen. Please contact me to arrange a viewing.*

*Yours sincerely,*

*Professor Mike O'Shaughnessy*

*P.S. Where exactly was it found?*

The email sent a thrill through his body. He knew the guy was just as excited as he was. His fingers hovered over the keyboard, not knowing what to write back or how much to reveal. When the kids got home from school, he was so distracted with after-school snacks and homework that it was only when he went online to do some further research that he noticed another email waiting in the inbox.

*Hello,*

*Not sure if you received my previous email. I would like to discuss your interesting find immediately. Please come to my office asap. Or ring me on my office number or mobile.*

Bryant's mouth went dry. Somehow he'd thought he could discreetly find out what he needed to know without having to meet up with anyone. As he sat at his laptop trying to work out the best way to proceed, there was an almighty bang on his front door. Bryant could just make out a bulky form through the frosted panels of glass, and when he opened the door there was a large man dressed in a fluoro-orange safety vest.

'Where's Kai's egg?'

'Sorry?' Bryant blinked. Then it came to him—his neighbour from across the road.

'I want Kai's egg.'

'What do you mean Kai's egg? My boys found it.'

'Bullshit. It's his.'

'It belongs to us.'

'I'll take youse to court.'

'Fine. Speak to my lawyer.'

Bryant pushed the door shut before the neighbour could wedge his leg inside. He could see the blurry shape of the man standing motionless and then he heard the buckling of metal as the figure gave the screen door two swift kicks.

'Dad?' Casey was standing beside him, with that look he gave when he didn't comprehend something.

'Kai's banned from coming over, right?'

'Why?'

'His dad claims the egg is his.'

'It's all of ours. Kai can have it one week, then us the next.'

'We're selling the egg.'

'Dad, no,' Casey pleaded. 'I don't want to sell it.'

Bryant snapped back, 'Do you want to go to Disneyland?'

'Yeah. I guess.'

'Then we're selling it.'

Casey started to protest, but stopped when he saw his dad's expression. Bryant knew what he had to do. He would get his wife to ring in sick for him, and then he'd keep a close watch over the egg until he could offload it to the highest bidder, and then maybe after that he'd better think about moving house.

\* \* \*

For the next three nights Bryant slept with the egg. He brought it in from the garage, and lay on the couch with the egg standing like a quiet sentinel beside him. The second evening he transferred it to the guest bedroom so he could get a better night's sleep but found himself waking with a start every hour or so just to check if the egg was still there. By the third night he had brought the egg into the bed with him, arm draped across it as he slept. Bryant's sleep was deep but troubled, infused with crazy dreams and an intense heat that spread from his body into the egg—or was it the other way around?—so that when he woke he was drenched in so much sweat he thought he had wet himself.

The situation was absurd, but he understood why he was so obsessed. *Skylab*. It was the year 1979 and there he was, a white-haired boy with scabs healing to pink on his knees, scrabbling through the scrub at the back of his house in search of pieces of the space station that had fallen through the milky night skies. He remembered the knobbly feel of honky nuts pushing into his cheap sneakers, and the fear of spiders as he pulled back fallen sheaths of papery bark, desperate to find anything foreign and metallic. And each night as he watched the Channel Seven news reports heralding the grinning kids and dads holding up their new-found bits of Skylab, he would glance across at his own dad, who sat with a beer on his belly and shoulders always on that downward slump.

Bryant eased himself out of bed, and hoisted the egg with him to the kitchen. It was Sunday morning, the quietest time in the household, and his wife was drinking her coffee with the laptop perched in front of her on the breakfast bar, browsing her favourite site: RealEstate.com.

'We can get a four bedroom, two bathroom with a pool and theatre room for only 750.'

Bryant frowned. 'We need to sell the egg first.'

'Have you contacted the museum guy yet? He's sent about another ten emails.'

'I'm still researching stuff.'

'What's that on your face?'

'What?'

'Those red marks.'

Bryant touched his cheek, and could feel a sea of lumps.

'Must have been bitten by something.'

'Dad, quick, you gotta see this.' Casey was wheezing as he came tearing into the kitchen. Bryant and his wife followed him outside to where their wheelie bin was positioned at the side of their house. The words 'Fuck You' were scrawled in white paint over the green bin.

'Who would do that?' whispered his wife.

'I know exactly who,' answered Bryant grimly.

'Is it that guy? He's been there all morning.' Casey pointed to a silver Mazda that was parked at the end of their cul-de-sac.

Bryant stared at the car, trying to make out the person sitting in the driver's seat. Suddenly they heard the pure, clear sound of a child's scream.

'Ben!' shouted his wife.

'The egg!' cried Bryant.

They all ran into the kitchen, to see the little boy wailing and rubbing his foot.

'It fell on my toe,' he whimpered.

'Didn't I tell you not to go anywhere near it,' yelled Bryant, making the boy cry even harder, his tiny shoulders quaking with each sob.

Bryant heaved the egg back into the guestroom, then went to peer through the front blinds. The silver Mazda had disappeared.

'It's just a coincidence,' he tried to tell himself, but he knew it was more likely that someone had tracked him down through his email account. The professor... Maybe, but there was also that bizarre exchange with Leonard58 on an antiquities forum, which had left him feeling unsettled.

'Ring the professor,' his wife urged him, and he knew that he could no longer hide in that no man's land of hope and longing.

* * *

His wife dropped him off in Northbridge at the Cultural Centre and Bryant hurried across the square with the egg wrapped loosely in the sheet. People stared. For all they knew he could have been an art student carrying his end of semester project, but he wasn't dressed in cool retro clothing or like someone with the promise of idle summers stretched before them. Instead, he looked like a bag of shit. Over-laundered, short-sleeved shirt his wife had bought him one Father's Day and a greasy stubble where he had smeared some cortisone over the itchy red lumps. At the front counter the museum staff eyed him with suspicion, until he told them he had an appointment with the professor.

He was expecting a man as dry and colourless as the specimens he curated; instead, this man before him was young and robust, with a rosy hue to his skin.

'Bryant. Good to meet you. Is this the...?' Professor O'Shaughnessy seemed to tremble as he touched the egg.

'Not here,' muttered Bryant.

'Of course. My office.'

Bryant followed the professor to the other side of the building, gripping the egg protectively.

'Let's look at it, shall we?' and the professor knelt down and unwrapped the giant specimen. He smoothed his hand over it, and examined it closely, turning it around slowly to study it from every angle. Bryant watched him for clues, trying to second-guess what he was thinking.

'I can't say for sure, but it looks like it's man-made.'

'What?' Bryant's heart began to race.

'Man-made. It's either ceramic or a type of metal casing.'

'It can't be.'

'I can do some further tests if you like. Ask my colleagues. Maybe a CT scan. You can leave it with me and I'll let you know.'

'Do you take me for an idiot?'

'I'm sorry?'

'An idiot. I'm not leaving the egg here so you can sell it yourself.'

'Have you not heard me?' The blotches of colour deepened across the professor's cheeks. 'It's not an egg. Someone's having a joke on you.'

Bryant stood up. He thought of a nine-year-old boy making a stance, a boy sticking it to the authorities by reburying the 2000-year-old egg in a secret location. He could do one better than that. One giant Fuck You. He grabbed the egg and brought it down with such force that it broke on impact with the ground, shattering like a meteorite in every direction. One piece flew into his leg and surprised him with the pain, another lodged in the professor's eye, which wept red like an anemone. Bryant ignored the cry, the blood beginning to trickle in lazy rivulets down his leg. He limped away, past the gallery and towards the station, knowing his forty seconds to work it all out would soon pass, leaving him with no better understanding; only the feel of the city sun on his skin bringing a healing warmth, the pulse and throb letting him know he was alive.

# THE RETURNING

The first time I saw my father cry was at the airport. My mother was distracted by a woman she vaguely knew, so there was a moment when it was just my father and me standing at the departures gate, and his long face, normally a fixture of calm rationality, crumpled a little then broke. I was so taken aback that later, on the way to Singapore and then Frankfurt Airport, whenever I thought of that moment where his face lost its familiar, rigid composure, I would also silently weep.

The year was 1983 and I was on my way to Germany for a twelve-month student exchange program. A year when children still dressed in pyjamas to greet family members in the Perth Airport arrivals hall and there was still a kangaroo enclosure near the car park, a family of bored roos with fly-bitten ears. A year when a graffiti-covered wall in Berlin still separated East from West.

This time, I leave on my own. My mother has been dead almost twenty-five years and my father is too infirm to make it to the airport to see me off. I look around, half expecting to see someone like my mother dressed in white elasticised pants, yelling, *Yoo-hoo, Ellie!*

This time, I don't need to race through Changi Airport to obtain a new boarding pass for the next leg of the journey to Frankfurt. Instead, I stay in the Qantas Business Lounge, grazing on the crackers and salads and reading the *Australian Financial Review*.

No-one will meet me in Frankfurt. I will make my own way by taxi then train to the town of Würzburg, and stay overnight in a hotel room. In the morning I will hire a car and then drive the 41.9 kilometres to the small village of Markt Bibart. I am counting on the fact that nobody there will recognise me. A lot has changed in thirty-four years. I am no longer plump and downy-cheeked, and my once flowing long, dark hair has been cropped and dyed to a shimmering grey. My dress sense has changed too. When I look at old photographs I can't remember what it was like to wear those floating pastel colours and patterned Indian scarves. Now I favour all black—structured jackets and tailored, dry-clean-only trousers—and silver bespoke jewellery: oversized rings with expensive stonework—my favourite being an amethyst worn on my ring finger, even though I'm no longer married. No-one here will be able to navigate this version of myself because they never saw this transformation happen. To them, I will be a complete stranger. Well, that's what I hope for, though to make sure of this I also wear dark Armani sunglasses as I drive the car through the tiny village's main street.

What strikes me at first is how much I don't remember. The place looks familiar in that way all German villages do: centuries-old houses built at odd angles and abutting the road so that it seems as if all the cars will veer into their cornerstones, the *fachwerk* whitewashed buildings with carved wooden flower boxes, and narrow cobblestone pathways. But I spend more time thinking about whether that Gasthaus was there before, or that public garden or that shop front. I wonder if it is because I am now driving, and not on foot, or leaning against a bus window, my eyes semi-shuttered, and my hand against my cheek, softening the bumps from the road. Or is that what trauma does to you, allows you to block out huge chunks of time so that those bumps are softened too? I drive on, following the GPS and looking for the fields of corn and the copse of woodland signalling where this village ends and the next one begins. I think there is a cemetery here somewhere—I have the sudden recollection of a story about an elderly couple whose only daughter was murdered in Nuremberg, her head hacked off while she was closing up the butcher shop one night in the Turkish district. This happened years before I first arrived, and the parents still made the daily pilgrimage to the graveside, lighting candles when the winter days shortened into night. Now I can't see a cemetery and I have no desire to type that destination into the GPS. I am here for the living, not the dead.

I recognise a stretch of road, the newer housing development built in the 1960s, and then a row of houses—and one in particular that makes me pull over and cut the engine. At this end of the street the double-storey homes are covered in cheap, prefabricated white cladding. Even time hasn't closed up the telltale seams.

The house is exactly as I remember it. There is still no garden to speak of. Just a strip of lawn in front of the lattice-topped fence, and a fir tree planted too close to the house, so that it looks as if it is trying to smother it with needled hands. There are frosted panels of brown glass on the front door, and windows of varying sizes on both storeys. The largest one upstairs is the kitchen, the smallest one downstairs a bathroom. But staring at the house I am now feeling confused. There isn't a level where a basement should be; I can see that the house abruptly stops at the ground. All these years I had remembered living in a basement, and as I push my brain into understanding this anomaly, I realise that by descending down the stairs after each meal to hide in my room it must have felt as if I was retreating to an even lower level of life.

I notice that all the blinds are raised, and just flimsy, netted curtains form a barrier between the inside and outside worlds. I could easily be seen by the inhabitants, so I slump further down in my car seat and continue to watch. My heart is doing strange things: rapid-fire beats and then a sickly wobble. I anchor my thoughts on the leather steering wheel and the solid ring I am twisting around on my finger. There is someone walking up the street, coming straight towards me, a small, slow-moving figure, and I suddenly realise that I have got the days of the week confused. It must be Friday, and it's Käthe walking to her cleaning job at the Seyfrieds', three doors down. Käthe, who pulled me into her house one day to show me the small pig she kept boarded up under the kitchen table. The poor creature squealed and butted its head against the rough planks of wood, and I watched in horror as Käthe thrust shrivelled cobs of corn in and out of its mouth in a teasing manner. All the while the pig crashing and grunting as Käthe laughed deep in her throat, her mouth a ruined black hole.

But it can't be Käthe, can it? I do the quick calculation and work out that she must be ninety-five now, or dead.

The person walks past my car and I see it is a boy of about eleven or twelve wearing shorts and a red soccer shirt. He turns to stare at me; a slow, deliberate, searching look. I don't recognise a thing about him—he could be a boy from anywhere in the world, even a boy in Australia. But it's a look that I instantly recognise: suspicion before it turns to a quiet loathing.

\* \* \*

I am driving to a different town, this time Scheinfeld, though now I keep calling it Seinfeld in my head. A bit of humour won't do me any harm. The countryside is beautiful, but I can't be distracted by the lush fields and the commanding castle that dominates the hill and skyline. I need to focus on driving on the right-hand side of the road and keeping my eyes open for anything meaningful. I need to buy some different clothes, something that will make me blend in more. I had forgotten how necessary it was to fit in. I follow the route marked out for me to the outskirts of town, and then slow down to find parking outside the clothing store. Obviously the latest discount shop to open up in Scheinfeld. But what does 'latest' mean? This store could have been here for the last twenty years.

The first thing that strikes me when I walk inside is the spiralling racks of sale items. The second thing that strikes me is that the racks are in the shape of swastikas. Surely this is a mistake? I head for the sections marked *Damen*, and rifle through the items, not knowing what I am looking for. A shop assistant comes up to me, a stunning girl with blonde highlighted hair and perfect honey skin.

'*Kann ich Ihnen helfen?*'

'*Ich brauche...* size 6 jeans.'

'Oh, you are American?'

'No. English,' I lie.

She scans my body. 'I will bring you size 8.'

I take a couple of items with me and follow her to the cubicle, where I get undressed. The clothes are completely wrong for my body shape, accentuate my big thighs and small breasts. It doesn't matter, I tell myself. I will dispose of them afterwards. I think about what was in fashion back then, the three distinctive looks: cord jeans and Fruit of the Loom shirts; the post-hippie flowing garments, where even the boys wore the Indian cotton scarves with their T-shirts—a look that still makes my heart lurch every time I see a man wearing a light cotton scarf; and then the *Trachten* revival. The girls knitting the tight-fitting cardigans during English class; cinched-in jackets to match their traditional Bavarian outfits. You needed bigger breasts for that look.

I keep the clothes on and go to the counter to pay for them. The shop attendant studies my hands. 'I like your rings.'

'*Danke*,' is all I can say.

Outside, the sky is so beautiful and the day so warm that I want to be like a lizard and bask in the sun. I think about buying some food and sitting in a park. Instead, I get into the car and start driving, not using the GPS but relying on some inner compass. I find myself passing restaurants and bakeries, and I keep driving until I stop outside the Gymnasium, the local high school. The main building is like a grey office block, but the taller front façade is rendered the whitest of white and has colourful geometric patterns painted all over it. I only remember the grey brick part. This is where I took classes in Year 13, the *Abitur* year, even though I had already graduated high school in Australia. The place where the Religion and Ethics teacher, Herr Strang, with his stringy hair and yellowed cat teeth, asked me what my religion was, and I answered in my newly minted German, *Vereinigte Kirche*. Uniting Church. And then something changed in his expression and he grabbed my arm and pulled me out to the front of the class, his voice full of invective and venom, and even with my imperfect German I knew I had been branded as dangerous.

There was nothing else for me to do but leave the classroom. Then I started running. I ran down the hallway headed for the safety of the girls' toilets and almost collided with Frau Lang, the Senior English teacher. Seeing my tears she steered me to an empty room and asked me what had happened.

'Ah,' she said slowly. 'You meant to say *Vereinigung der Kirche*. The *Uniting* Church, not *Unification* Church. That is the Moonies cult.'

Frau Lang with the comforting overstretched woollen pullovers, green tweed skirts, thick black stockings and sensible moccasins. She was the only teacher I liked—and who I thought liked me, until I worked out she only spent time with me in order to practise her English.

I've begun shivering, so I turn on the ignition and keep driving through the older part of town. I look for the café where I spent hours in clouds of cigarette smoke, eating plum pastries whilst wagging school. Now I crave buttery, flaky pastry, and would kill for a cigarette despite the fact I haven't smoked since university days. I turn down Kirche Strasse, and this is so familiar that it hurts to see it. There is the post office, where once a month I would stand inside the private wooden phone booth at the back of the room dialling a number, and feeding coins into the metal slot as if it was a hungry beast. There'd be a click and then the sound of the coins falling, metal raining upon metal, and my mother's muffled voice like she was trapped at the bottom of the ocean, *Hello luv*, the familiarity setting me off into a convulsion of sobs. And the two postal workers, men in their fifties with dyed black hair and bellies hoisted over tight belts, calling out something in German after I had finished talking. *Do you want to go out drinking?*

Suddenly I want to park the car and go inside and find that same old-fashioned phone set and ring the same number. A part of me wants to believe that my mother will still be alive, sitting on the damped-down furrows of the ocean floor, and will pick up one more time.

\* \* \*

I keep on driving. I see a sign which says *Freibad*, and translate it literally, Free Bath, although I know it is the sign for the open-air swimming pool. The trick is not to do the translation word for word, but to allow the German to exist as if there is no other option. I never learned this, nor did I dream in German as promised. But I developed a stutter; my tongue got stuck on the thick army of consonants and the *ichs* were like a fishbone caught at the back of my throat.

I see a forest ahead, and slow down to see if there is somewhere to park. I pull into a section of unsealed road, and park next to an empty van. There are numerous trails to be followed, each path littered with brown, powdery pine needles. I need to stretch out my cramped legs and make the most of this unscheduled break. I stride along, able to see great distances ahead, as there is no undergrowth, just tree poles and long-legged shadows. The day has warmed up and with every footfall more of the fragrance of the forest is released.

This forest reminds me of that holiday place. A village in the north on the East German border, which I have forgotten the name of. All I know is that it felt like we were driving for hours on the fast-moving autobahn while I slept in the back of the car as if I were the family dog. Each day I walked the forest trails on my own, and the unexpected blush of wild raspberries and the sweet trill of birdsong weren't enough to break through my darkness. And then one day, when walking along a different path, I emerged into cleared farmland and saw the high wire-mesh fence and a large sign: *Achtung! Zonengrenze!* There was no need to translate this into English. Set about fifty metres back from the border line was a tall lookout tower, a relic from the cold war: an enclosed metal and glass hut with a viewing platform and a single outer ladder. By narrowing my eyes I could make out the shape of a guard inside the hut staring back at me through one of the three panelled windows. I stood for ages watching the guard, and then, not knowing why, I raised a hand and waved at him, and then I saw him waving back. A thrill cut through me like ice, a sensation so swift and invigorating that I craved to feel it again. The next day and the next, I returned to the very same spot to wave at the guard, but he never waved back, just stood there watching as I inched closer and closer to the border fence.

Now I am walking through a different forest but it could be the same. Same forest, different girl. I want to remember what it is like to be cleaved by ice. I think about the guard and wonder if he is still alive, and what it was like for him to finally cross over the border when East and West were reunited. And would he remember the girl who stood there waving, so brazen and free, moving closer and closer to the fence in a dangerous dance, not knowing whether she wanted to be loved or shot?

I keep on walking and see two figures up ahead. As they approach me I can see it is two men, and one is carrying a long, metallic object. At first I think it is a rifle, but then as they pass, I can see that it is an oversized camera lens, the sort serious photographers use. They give me a cursory nod, and say, '*Grüss Gott.*' I translate it immediately in my head. Greetings from God.

They expect the same from me, but I can't say the words. There is nothing good or holy about today.

\* \* \*

## THE RETURNING

I am back in Markt Bibart, sitting in my hired car with my eyes trained on the house. The sun has moved to that point in the sky that makes you feel the day is already done. Summer time throws me; it feels like late afternoon now, when it's actually seven o'clock at night. I watch the largest top floor window for the slightest of movements. This is where the people will be having dinner, sitting at the built-in breakfast table with the home-made straw dolls dressed in traditional *Trachten* lined up along the sill. Although the dolls have no faces, they still have the uncanny ability to watch your every movement.

Some of the houses in the street have their blinds already drawn shut. The louvres are like eyelids, they open and shut, choosing to see what they want. I remember walking along this street and imagining the people at the windows as fat, dilating pupils that widened suddenly when they saw me or Herr Schulz's newly acquired, mail-order Thai bride, who he paraded like a sex toy.

The occupants will probably be having their *Abendbrot* by now. There is a mechanical bread cutter hidden in a cupboard, which will slice the bread in perfect width to accompany the evening cheese and the cold cuts. This is what I ate each night and what fattened me up, not unlike Käthe's poor imprisoned pig. Most nights the family would finish dinner and retire to the sitting area to watch television, or the kids would go to their bedrooms to do their homework, while I descended to my downstairs lodgings.

On occasion, when the father had too much beer, and the capillaries in his nose were fit to burst, he would invite me to stay at the kitchen alcove. Placing a bottle of wine and a bowl of nuts in front of me, he would begin his discussion about politics, NATO and the rise of Petra Kelly and the Greens Party, *Die Grünen*. Nothing in my German classes back home prepared me for such conversation; there was no opportunity to talk about the whereabouts of a train station or how the linden trees are reflected in a mirror-smooth lake. So my only contribution was to eat the nuts and drink the sickly sweet wine, saying all the while, '*Eben. Eben. Eben.*' Exactly. Exactly. Exactly.

This failure to speak still haunts me. Another failure to add to the list. Like the trip to the Berlin conference in summer, where I'd met up with the other exchange students from around the world: the Australians spiralling in for their first official camp, and the northern hemisphere students spiralling out, their undying adoration for *Mutti* and *Papa* still hot on their lips. West Berlin—where it felt like I was the only person overwhelmed by the multi-floored shopping Mecca KaDeWe, the galah-pink drinks at city street bars, and the frenzied dancing on nightclub floors fashioned like giant silver ashtrays. And then crossing over to the eastern side of the wall, and seeing how the colour was instantly sucked out of the air, the same kind of drabness everywhere—the same dull shop fronts, the same coats, the same cuts of meat, the same generic-brown wash of peasantry. And then knowing that when you return back to the glittering west, to the kaleidoscope of technicolour, it will be the same monochrome sky that will follow you wherever you go.

There is movement now at the window, shapes shifting as if in a mood lamp. It could be the mother of the house, bending over to clear the table. It might be the husband, standing to slap another slice of salami on his bread. In any case I have done my due diligence: I know the family still lives in this house. The mother would be a similar age to my own mother if she was still alive, though they couldn't have been more different in appearance and temperament. Frau Bauer, a large-boned woman with hair lacquered into a platinum helmet—nothing soft or generous about her, nothing gentle in the way she wiped the table down around me, leaving a little circle of dirt around my hands, while I stayed talking with her husband. And her twelve-year-old daughter, Konstanze, a clone of her mother, her giant spy eye searching my room for clues: the chocolate wrappers hidden under my bed; the stack of English novels piled up like contraband; the dead insects in the bath-tub, their mothy wings turning to dust.

I want to cry now for the girl who was stuck in that downstairs room, but she feels like a fiction to me. I begin to doubt that she ever existed. I feel, with every passing year, the skin cells being shed and replaced miraculously with something else. It is far easier to believe that girl is gone than to know she is still there, buried beneath calcified layers of scar tissue and time.

\* \* \*

I must have fallen asleep. I notice a missed call from my father and plan to phone him later, at a time when I can breathe energy again into his frail frame, keeping him alive more for me than him. There is a crick in my neck where my head has leaned at an unnatural angle against the car window. It feels like I am on a plane: my legs are cramped and restricted by the steering wheel and the too-tight jeans. I am cold, yet my nostril breath is mare-hot, misting up all the windows. I draw two circles in the driver's side to look out of, and see that it is light outside. A new day. I adjust the rear-view mirror, and examine my face in the darkling glass. Yesterday's makeup is wearing thin, and cannot disguise the deep lines on my forehead and around my lips. I should have come here ten years ago when I was at my peak, but there was always this thought recycled in my head: You can always be prettier, thinner, richer... The two circles act as inadequate binoculars. There is this sense that I am missing something else out there, smeared under the mist. I enlarge the left-hand eye circle, and can see some people in the distance leaving a house. Why so early? And I wonder if it is Sunday and I've lost another day, and they are off to one of the churches in the village—the only choice being that narrow doorway between Catholic and Lutheran.

I am so intent on trying to see where they are going that I fail to see the door of my own house open and the people spilling out. Now it is too late to gird myself for what I have come to do, and the family have spotted the car and they are walking over to me. I grope the seat next to me as I keep my eyes trained on the four figures, blindly trying to find my pair of sunglasses, my useless disguise. They are almost at the car, and there is nothing to do but meet them face on, through the two circles of light. My two eyes, and their eight staring back at me. I wait for that flicker of recognition, and when it comes, my right hand reaches for the ignition and my foot hits the floor hard. Before I know it, I am accelerating as if at the speed of light, driving away from pointed fingers and words on the wind. I keep on driving until I reach the safety of the outskirts of town and idle at the intersection, my ticking heart the only sound in the still car.

The logical part of my brain knows they are not the same family. The mother and father are far too young to even be the host children, and their dark hair and skin and their short stature do not match the family DNA profile. The name 'Bauer' must be more common than I think.

*Thirty-four years in the waiting*, and I feel cheated. No chance to prepare for that right moment, to turn on my iPhone and show them the photos of my riverside apartment, nor open up my LinkedIn profile to reveal my impressive career. No chance to wipe out any trace of that girl at the Bavarian districts' dinner, the girl who stood in front of the club members and their wives with her stuttering slide show of Perth. The kangaroo paws, the black swans, the fallen soldiers at Kings Park, the fake Tudor of London Court. Wipe out the disappointment of the host family as they remember the procession of the other clubs' students who came before her—the fresh-faced beauties blowing kisses to sweet koalas, the impossibly blue skies over Sydney Harbour. The dawning realisation that they got the raw end of the deal, the B-side of the record.

I want to see how their lives stayed small whilst mine opened up wider than the Indian Ocean. But now I realise that they, too, must have moved on: to bigger cities, to better houses, giving birth to the next generation of taller and smarter Bauers. And Germany has moved on, too. There's a new version of Germany, one without any borders, welcoming all who seek safety and refuge, and with greater religious freedoms than simply Lutheran or Catholic. The old Germany has been laid to rest, just like the politician Petra Kelly, shot in the head while she lay sleeping.

Maybe it would have been enough just to sit in the car staring up at that window, touching my tongue against the roof of my mouth, fashioning 'fuck you' silently, the same way I do in board meetings when the men speak over me.

A small farmhouse catches my eye. This I know. It is set apart from all the other houses in the village and its walls are falling down, crumbling away to nothingness. Thick, glossy ivy has crept out of the eaves and has papered over the missing stonework. I can still picture Käthe pottering about in the derelict kitchen dressed in her dirty work pinafore.

Ladling the giant *Klösse* onto the plate and pouring the thick gravy over them so that their gelatinous shapes quiver and take on the meaty flavours. I feel safe in this warm kitchen now that the pig is gone and is no longer bashing its frantic head beneath the table. Käthe's kindnesses are a welcome gift. She lets me stay until school is officially over and I can wander the village streets without scrutiny. Now she is bringing out something from a secret drawer set into the table. It is a Nazi propaganda pamphlet with a picture of a young German girl on the cover, a pretty girl with wheaten braids and dressed in a uniform. *Bund Deutscher Mädel*, League of German Girls. She says something to me in guttural Bavarian, and the words are as thick as an officer's coat. And I just stare into that dark tunnel of her mouth, stare and stare, and it goes on without end.

# MONKEY PUPPET

If it wasn't for the Children's Ministry conference, the monkey puppet would have remained flopped at the back of the church storeroom, next to the fuzzy felt board and the Noah's Ark kits with the missing instructions. Elizabeth had been going to the annual conference for years, seeing the same presenters fire up their powerpoints, the predictable assortment of craft and CDs for sale in the foyer, and the same friendly (mainly female) attendees from the different Baptist churches in Perth: the younger ones, fresh and dewy cheeked, and the older ones, hanging on for dear glory. And the same obese girl, rushing to the stage whenever a volunteer was called for (how many years had Elizabeth seen her do that?); a heaving, wobbling effort to mount the four steps, and everyone clapping and cheering, as if she was being congratulated for just being fat.

But this year was different. A man in his thirties from Melbourne dressed in jeans, leading a seminar on the art of puppetry. His passion wasn't the usual shouting kind, with a voice modulated to a child's pitch when making something sound pithy and catchy. No, his was a casual delivery bordering on boredom, which made the audience quieten their breathing, and lean forward as if they were readying themselves for the start of a race.

Puppetry was a science, the young man explained. Easily broken down into key guiding principles. A mystery that master puppeteers like Jim Henson had instinctively known, and could now be taught to someone like Elizabeth. He demonstrated by way of a sock. An ordinary, everyday sock—like the kind her late husband had worn to his job in the council offices, and then in the retirement years with his sandals and shorts.

And applying these logical, scientific principles, Elizabeth watched in amazement as the garment—an indeterminate blend of viscose and Egyptian cotton—took on a hilarious and engaging personality that seemed to have nothing to do with the bland-looking young man from Melbourne.

Of course, the puppeteer was the star of the conference. People clamoured afterwards to share their own experience with puppetry, to ask questions about characterisation or how they could customise their disappointing store-bought puppets. Elizabeth didn't feel the need to talk. She couldn't wait to get home and try it for herself. A sock wasn't an option though. Her own socks were too short, and designed for the days when she still played tennis. And as soon as she put on one of her husband's socks, it shocked her to see the triangles of the pattern distort and thin out over her plump arm, instead of the pleasing tartan that used to scale her husband's skinny, ropy calves.

That's when she thought about the old monkey puppet. So the next day she drove out to her church, found it amongst the discarded, broken things in the storeroom, and brought it back to her small unit, to work with in private.

The first thing to do was to strip off the monkey's flat-disc eyes and replace them with halved ping-pong balls. That's what the young man had said. *Always get rid of the factory-made two-dimensional eyes.* Then Elizabeth grabbed a thick black texta and circled in some pupils, making sure she followed the principle of the Magic Triangle—where the darkest point of each eye leads to the tip of the puppet's nose, thereby drawing the audience in.

Already the monkey looked more engaging, so she slipped her hand into the puppet's head to test it out but faltered, not knowing what to do next. She thought about the young man's words: *Choose a puppet's personality opposite to your own.* So she attempted a comic jig and a loud, cackling laugh, and then let the puppet quickly fall away from her wrist, for it felt thoroughly alien and wrong.

\* \* \*

Elizabeth was determined, though, not to give up. Later on, she put the puppet back on her hand and stood in front of her bedroom mirror, practising moving the monkey's jaws like a hinge so they opened straight, making sure she didn't push the head artificially forward. For each word, Elizabeth mimicked the syllables' length, widening the monkey's mouth on the longer ones.

'I want a cook-ie, I want a cook-ie,' she repeated, until she felt she had mastered this action. She began to understand what the young man was saying. Puppets need to speak and move like real people, not like our imagined idea of how a puppet should act. As she walked around her kitchen putting away dishes, or out to her small patio to check the dryness of her pots, the monkey's hairy arms stayed linked around her neck and one of her hands remained inside its orange felt mouth. And she understood why the mouth had to be soft—not wooden or plastic, but able to be pliable in her fingers so she could manipulate the felt and create the slight expression of timidity, a crumpled, rumpled resignation, or her favourite: eating lemons!

By Sunday, she was finally ready to bring George (the name she'd chosen) to a wider audience. Or an abridged version of George, for the young man had told them that if the puppeteer wasn't totally confident in bringing the puppet alive, then it could be brought to the stage and used simply as a prop.

Elizabeth arrived early to the church so that she could photocopy the extra colouring-in sheets and set up her lesson. The pastor's wife had left her usual note about stacking the chairs and making sure the tables were wiped clean of glitter and glue. She checked the roster. One parent helper was listed: Sue Ong, the mother of two girls, their sleek bobs cut like perfect curtains around their pretty faces. As she organised the room, Elizabeth could hear the troubled notes of the band rehearsing in the main auditorium.

What does it matter, she thought, as she put out the sign-in sheets listing the children's names, including those who had been permanently scratched off. Part of her was glad that the Sunday school class was shrinking in size—it was less work and far easier for her to manage—and yet the other part despaired when she felt the sum of all the empty spaces around her. She noticed that most of the names left on the list were Asian. A new type of faithful brought into the eastern suburbs of Perth. The parents were polite and smiling (some even bowed), and their children were shy and respectful, the girls' hair clipped with yellow plastic bows and the boys' shorts and shirts ironed in perfect creases. But when left with Elizabeth for two hours, the hair began to unravel, stains appeared on the dresses and the boys fashioned guns out of the fluoro click-it textas.

Today would be different. She had George. Already he hung around her neck, and when the children and their parents started to file in, there was wide-eyed wonder as the children stared at the monkey and back to each other. Of course they became noisy again when the parents left, except for Sue Ong's two children who sat like perfect bookends on either side of their mother. Usually Elizabeth would raise her voice, and force a false energy into her words, but today she sat quietly on a chair, manipulating the monkey so that it whispered into her ear. It had an immediate calming effect on the children, and they leaned forward to hear what was being said.

'Do you want to know what George just told me?' The children all nodded. 'He wants me to tell you a story.' George gazed at his audience, the ping-pong ball eyes and Magic Triangle doing their trick. 'What is it, George?' The monkey was whispering again into Elizabeth's ear. 'No, George. You can't tickle the children.'

Some of the children shrieked with delight and Aaron, the Malaysian boy who was faultless with his memory verses but also rude and disruptive each week, jumped up to pull the monkey off Elizabeth's neck. Without thinking she gave him three whacks with the puppet's head. The children laughed and Elizabeth said, 'Naughty, George. I thought you wanted to *tickle* the children.'

Elizabeth could see Aaron falter, a pink mark surfacing on his olive cheek, but he saved face by doing a clumsy half-cartwheel, and ending up in a crouched position to the left of the puppet. Elizabeth held her breath, glanced across to Sue Ong, who was smiling and nodding with her two small girls. George seemed to be a success. Elizabeth was able to finish her Bible story, with the occasional interruption from George, who whispered the things that only naughty children thought. At craft time, she put George away in a box and the lesson became the usual chaotic mess again. When it was time to pack away, and Elizabeth was collecting the leftover paper plates (they had made lion masks to match the Daniel story), Sue Ong thanked her, saying, 'So funny... So funny.'

When Elizabeth got home she was too wired to have her usual after-lunch nana nap. She felt the exhilaration of success (or was it the Holy Spirit?) as she kept replaying the morning's events over and over in her head.

\* \* \*

Every Friday Elizabeth met her sister Naomi for lunch, sometimes at a riverside café, sometimes at the newest city haunt for office workers. It didn't matter where: her sister always paid, pulling out her salmon-coloured leather wallet and the gold Mastercard. Today, it was a slick café on King Street with a blackboard-menu wall and waitstaff dressed like stagehands. For some unknown reason, Elizabeth had brought George along in her tote bag, and when they had ordered and there was that stretch of time when they usually relayed news about their grown-up children or latest doctor's appointments, Elizabeth brought out the monkey and laid him on the table. He was wearing a home-made tartan waistcoat which pinched in at his waist and clashed with the colour of his fur, giving him more of a raffish, comical look.

'That's not for me, is it?' her sister asked, quite capable of making a gift seem a burden.

'Meet George.' Elizabeth picked the puppet up and plied his mouth into a rude pucker.

'Is it for Bec's girls?'

'No, for Sunday school,' said Elizabeth, not wanting to explain that her daughter, Bec, rarely brought the girls around any more and seemed to favour her mother-in-law for babysitting, who could comfortably fit two booster seats in the back of a Subaru.

'Oh, my God. You're turning into Arthur!' Naomi gave the words the same weight they would carry if she'd accused her youngest sister of being a liar.

'No, I'm not.'

'Remember Charlie? Remember *that* doll?' As Naomi leaned her head forward, Elizabeth could see the freshly dyed roots, and the large smooth expanse of forehead that hardly moved.

'Charlie was a ventriloquist doll. George is a...' she paused for the right word. 'He's a Muppet, like the ones Jim Henson created. And he doesn't talk, he just whispers things to me.'

'As long as you're not doing an Arthur.'

The food was delivered to their table, slivers of protein lost in an airy, frilled salad, and probably costing as much as a steak dinner. Elizabeth wanted to enjoy the meal but she felt a sick sensation rise, leaving a familiar coppery taste, like old coins, in her mouth. Her sister talked about Easter plans and cruises with her husband, but Elizabeth couldn't find her way back from that comment, from Uncle Arthur, her mother's restless sailor brother who slept periodically on the cot in their sleepout when he visited between naval tours of the Pacific. Each time, he came bearing gifts for the girls: carved coconut bikini bras, whittled bamboo whistles, and their favourite, a Japanese doll encased in a large glass box, her blue kimono stiff like sails on a skiff, and her skin, a deathly, dense cloth. The last time Arthur stayed, coming back through Fremantle Port before his honourable discharge took him permanently east, he carried a case no bigger than a child's coffin. Inside, cushioned in purple satin, lay a wooden ventriloquist dummy with a painted, oily jaw.

*Meet Charlie*, he had said, bringing the doll, rigid and ill at ease, to his knee as he tried hard to synchronise the clanking joints and yackety-yack jaw. How could Elizabeth forget the next two weeks, as her uncle sat bare-chested in his navy shorts, clenching his teeth to trap the words, and all the time practising, *'Ello 'oys and girls. 'Ello 'oys and girls.*

The ginger hairs on his chest a curious curl, and her sister pushing Elizabeth forward—the youngest—so she would have to sit on his other knee and feel the hard plane of bone and hear the sound of that dreadful lacquered jaw.

It shouldn't matter, this comment about Arthur. The doll had long since been buried with her uncle in a lonely cemetery in Whyalla: two coffins lowered side by side into the grave, watched by her mother and the handful of cousins he had entertained over the years.

Naomi's voice broke into her thoughts. 'Do you remember the Japanese doll? The one in the glass case?'

'Whatever happened to that doll? I loved it!'

And then the mood suddenly brightened, the relief flooded the room, and they began to reminisce about their own versions of the past, adding piecemeal to each other's memories, making Elizabeth wonder if this was the only thing that made their time together really matter, and why being a sister worked more often than it did not.

\* \* \*

Elizabeth kept bringing the monkey puppet to church, sometimes even arriving through the main entry doors with him already swinging off her neck. The children loved George—adored him!—and could not get enough of his unpredictable ways. Even Elizabeth was surprised by what he would do next, the unscripted part of the lesson where she would allow flashes of inspiration to lead her puppet hand, and the unplanned little tics and bursts that personified George. He seemed to become naughtier, interrupting Elizabeth with insistent whispers as she told the Bible story, and hitting, even biting, the children. The room was so loud with howls and screams that the parent helper had to close the glass doors so that the worshippers in the main hall wouldn't be drowned out by all the noise.

One day, the little Ong girls dressed in matching Korean lace were scratched by George's left eye, the plastic on the ping-pong ball having become slightly cracked and jagged. This time Sue Ong didn't smile or bow, when signing out her girls, but lowered her eyes so they disappeared into her luminous face.

The pastor's wife came marching in with a warning.

'Elizabeth, there have been complaints. You're hurting the children.'

'It's just a bit of fun. The children love George.'

'I think it's time to lose the puppet,' the woman cautioned. 'You can't bring children to Christ through a monkey.'

Elizabeth wanted to remind her about the times God spoke through a tax collector, or through a prophet's loquacious donkey, but instead she squeezed her lips into a pursed bow. As did George.

Let your puppets do what puppets do best, wasn't that the philosophy of the art of puppetry? There was George—all lanky and fuzzy with the whimsy of a misshapen head—and then there was Elizabeth, wearing her custom crimplene sleeves to mask the sag at the top of her arms, and the deep creases fanning like shark gills from the corners of her mouth.

\* \* \*

Elizabeth's new idea came to fruition when she was thinking about Bec. The time when her daughter was about eighteen months old, a chubby child struggling to toddle, but with the weight of the fat nappy holding her back. Television was new to the household, a luxury even in black and white, and one day in desperation Elizabeth plonked the child onto a potty in front of the TV. A children's show was playing, with bears and clowns and a pretty girl who couldn't act or sing. But it didn't matter to Bec, who sat entranced by it all, happy to watch whatever was contained and framed by the monstrous wood-veneer box. Inspired by this memory, Elizabeth set to work creating her own set. She picked up a refrigerator box from Harvey Norman, cut the top off and painted the whole thing black. She would change the act, give George a script, a stage, a voice—*freedom*—pry him from her neck and allow him to roam.

It was a lot of work, what with finding and making props and practising the script word for word, so that by Sunday morning Elizabeth felt completely drained. When the children started to arrive at 9.15, she was already hidden in her box. She couldn't see out (a distinct disadvantage of this style of theatre), but she could hear some excited chatter and children being led to the seats by the parent helper. She felt the nervous energy flutter in her chest—and then she was ready, pushing George high, so that he popped up wondrously from the box, dressed as a little Jesus. She bobbed him along the theatrette's edge, making sure she held the puppet at the same height the whole time to maintain the proper illusion of legs.

''Ello boys and girls. Today's story is about how I calmed the seas...' There was a stunned silence as the children heard George's squeaky and shrill voice for the first time.

Elizabeth had placed her props in order: there was the boat, the blue cellophane representing the Sea of Galilee, plastic fish, a net, and two teddies who were to be John and Peter. But as the story unfolded, with Elizabeth working, as if a blind person, to get the props quickly up and down, things soon became out of sync, and without this scripted order she lost her way. She was supposed to finish with a song about believing in miracles but her arm ached, and she could barely manage to hold George upright, let alone make him sing and jig. Through the dank painted cardboard, she could sense the fidgety boredom, the silence before the storm. Suddenly she felt a tug on her hand, like a fish taking a bold bite, and then George's body slipped away as if he was being swept out to sea. Alarmed, Elizabeth emerged from the box to see Aaron shaking the poor monkey, swinging its arms about like a broken windmill.

'Stop that!'

Elizabeth grabbed the puppet and began to whip the small boy, flailing him with the monkey's skinny arms, stinging him with fabric, until she saw the boy cower down, hands protecting his head. An eerie silence stilled the room. It was the quietest it had ever been. Elizabeth looked around and, to her astonishment, saw only a couple of children sitting in the chairs. Hidden away in her black box she hadn't realised there was hardly any audience today; most of the children, like the pretty Ong girls, were long gone.

Elizabeth excused herself, left the few remaining children with some colouring-in sheets and the monkey puppet in a scrappy heap on the floor. She walked out to the church storeroom where the old stuff was still being hoarded—the broken crèche toys, the embroidered Fruits of the Spirit wall-hanging, the artificial flowers in urns. All the items that no-one could bear to throw away. Long wooden church pews were double banked against the walls, having been replaced in the hall years ago by rows of durable plastic. She remembered the days as a child when the elderly gentlemen would totter bow-limbed down the aisles, take off their hats, then bend and slide their trousered legs across the polished pews. Now, it hurt to slide her own legs across the splintered, neglected wood, but she preferred it that way. After all, forgiveness was like going against the rough grain. Allowing your sister to push you forward, towards the sailor man with one hand up a puppet, the other up a skirt—your eyes wobbling and rattling like a dummy's, as your insides scream out red.

# ARROW

Each morning Fran holds her breath to see whether her son has made it through another night. The empty packet of Arnott's Savoury Shapes is a good sign. Also, the slops of curry at the base of the fridge. Now she is able to start getting ready for her day at work.

Before she leaves the house, she places a packet of Tim Tams inside the fridge to keep them cool. She thinks about writing a note, but decides against it. The last one, she found ground to a pulp in the dishwasher. She wonders if Damien is still wearing the same tartan blanket poncho, with a hole hacked in the centre to make room for his fat neck. Or whether his skin is still as pale as the cabbage moths that flutter like paper over the tomato bushes.

Fran likes to think of her son as a harmless resident ghost, sexless and sweet like Casper, not the angry, unwashed twenty year old who has stewed for years in his own filth.

\* \* \*

'You're the classic enabler,' says Coral Knightley, Head of the English Department, who always holds court on the softest sofa in the staffroom. Coral is wrong. Fran can't think of a single thing that Damien is able to do, apart from retracing the small arc of his life: a few steps to his room, the fridge, the toilet. Oh, there was that one time she had found the front door unchained and left ajar—does that count?—the thought of him stepping out in the early hours of the morning onto the dark front porch, blinking at the neighbouring yards of nothingness.

Coral leans forward to rub Fran on the arm, and slows her voice to a child's pace. 'He needs to leave home. Stand on his own two feet.'

Fran is beginning to tire of Coral and her regular psychobabble. The other staff members aren't much help either. Fran suspects they only listen in so they can feel better about themselves, like people who watch those hoarding horror shows. She excuses herself from Coral's condescending hand, and takes her lunch box to her office at the end of the hallway.

She eats hunched over her desk and bits of dry rice fall between the computer keys. There is dust on the computer screen and small sprinkles of dander on the black base. When Fran is at work, the arc of her day becomes smaller, too, like Damien's: the car park, the staffroom, her desk. It's been months since she organised a careers seminar for the students or a vocational pathways talk for the parents. The last district Careers Expo she attended was two years ago in June, when she'd sat at a booth stacked with copies of the *Job Guide* and watched the students bypass her stall and flock to another decked out in colourful balloons and a psychedelic hand-painted sign: Free Personality Testing.

Fran looks out of her window at the neatly edged chapel garden and the row of cars with P-plates in the car park. She can just make out her small yellow Datsun, a lonely canary amongst the dazzling sea of silver and white. Spotto, she says in her head, just like Damien would have said at the age of ten. A gardener moves a wheelbarrow slowly over the lawn, and Fran wonders if the girls—or boys—have a crush on him. Find him *hot*. She remembers what it is like to go to an all-girl school and develop crushes on the unlikeliest of people. The effeminate Japanese teacher, the pock-cheeked bus driver. But these girls seem different, more confident and more certain of all their options. They wouldn't settle for a gardener. It reminds her of the series of career bullseye charts from the Department of Education, tacked all over her office walls to add a semblance of colour. Career options for every subject imaginable: maths, science, history, English—even a chart for entertainment. All the colourful rings of possibility, inner and outer, and you shoot for the best possible life.

*Bullseye!*

\* \* \*

Fran listens to Amy Hepple talk on and on, and wonders if she is an alien. Her eyes are too widely spaced, like a bug, and she has an impossibly high forehead. And there is a blue-green vein in her forehead that could be the conduit for all that alien blood, the mother source of this über-ambition. For Amy wants to be a CEO by the time she's thirty, Amy wants to be as famous as Mark Zuckerberg. There's no point in even showing Amy Hepple the bullseye because her career trajectory is clearly off the charts.

Fran can hear the next Year Ten student shuffling electricity on the carpet outside her door. She needs to cut Amy short but Amy doesn't pause for a breath, she just goes on and on and on. Fran dislikes the girl but watching her is addictive, so she lets her speak about the Duke of Edinburgh's Award and her volunteer job at the Nulsen Haven Foundation and wonders what it would be like to live inside Amy's forehead. Or anyone's head for that matter. Who can *really* know someone unless you prise open their skull cage and step inside? A baby would know though, wouldn't they? Absorbing more than just nutrients through the womb wall: the mother's thought patterns, silent conversations, the nervous beats of the hand and the heart.

With Damien's father it was different, inside Fran for less than thirty seconds.

Fran looks beyond Amy's head at the rows and rows of cars. Two of the Year Twelve students are fooling around against a silver car, then they lean playfully across the bonnet, the girl on top of the boy, and her long shimmering ponytail spills like a waterfall over his face. From this distance it's hard to see if they are kissing, or mouths brushed together and laughing, but Fran can imagine it: the surprising softness of the touching lips, the mint and tang of saliva and lip balm and then an unnameable earthen taste that comes from beyond the throat, from deep within a beating chest. The students pull away from each other, and there is a moment where they seem frozen in time, blinded by the ripples of light that shoot across the metallic hoods and bonnets, little flying arrowheads, and Fran feels weirdly cold, as if one has flown through her heart. The students suddenly come alive again, warm up in the sun's steady rays and then they race up the stairs, their hips softly bouncing together along the pathway to the chapel. Fran recognises them by the way they move: Kyra has plans to be a dancer, Ryan a sports physio.

'Do you have a boyfriend?' The words seem to leap out from nowhere.

Fran sees Amy hesitate. This is obviously not the kind of question she has prepared for in her short sprint to the top.

'My son... If you're interested...' Fran's voice falls away as she notices Amy's widening black pupils. A shocked, sickened expression, as if the moon has settled permanently over the sun.

Fran knows now that the students have heard and believed all the stories about Damien. Or is it just her, Fran, who they know and despise?

'That's all,' says Fran sharply. 'No need to see me again. According to Myers-Briggs, your type is destined to rule the world.'

\* \* \*

Coral has cornered Fran in the staff bathroom again. She bangs on about a story that Fran is certain she's heard before. Either watching a TED podcast or reading it in a Steve Biddulph book about raising boys. It's a modern-day retelling of the 'Jack and the Beanstalk' fairy tale, where instead of the mother throwing the beans in the garden, she gently takes them and locks them in the dark cupboard, saying to her son, *We'll discuss this in the morning*.

'See,' says Coral, twisting her lips in a smug fashion. 'If the mother had been angry and thrown the beans in the garden, then Jack would've had his adventure, slayed the giant and become the man he was destined to be.'

Fran wonders if Coral talks like this at home to her husband. Probably not. With her grown-up children dotted around the country, there are only the Year Twelve English students and she who are Coral's remaining captives.

'Sorry, I'm in a hurry. Gotta fly.'

Fran flees the building, and escapes in her car. On the way home she pulls into the Bunnings car park, something she does whenever she feels the anxiety take hold. The warehouse looks empty, only a few tradies and retirees looking for the right screw or nail for the job. Fran makes her way to the paint section and stands in front of the Dulux colour selections. There they are, little slips of the rainbow fanning out from one colour spectrum into the next. All those endless possibilities. She runs her fingers along a row of blue and takes every fifth sample out, then folds them away in her purse. A big lad with baggy jeans and a store name badge, 'Dean', watches her, but pretends not to notice. He's seen her too many times to think she's shopping for paint. She is stealing colour. Dean's face is flushed, like a permanent sunburn, a perfect match for his prickled reddish hair.

Fran wonders about his educational background, how he seems a little slow and slack-jawed, and whether Damien, too, could work in a place like this. She remembers the first summer when they bought their house after years of renting, and how they spent countless weeks taking home the sample pots, testing stripe upon stripe of blue all over his bedroom wall. And how they laughed at the names, laughed so much it hurt their breastbones—Snorkel Sea, Mineral Mist, Cousteau—and then coming up with their own versions of colour: Mystic Bruise, Sneezy Breezy and Varicose Vein. *That's a cool job, to name the Dulux paints*, he'd said, and Fran pictured Damien, so happy thinking up the new names as if he was Adam christening all the animals at the beginning of Creation. And the snatches of joy continued for them in unexpected bursts—at the hairdresser or in cream-walled waiting rooms, when Damien would lean over to whisper in her ear, *Mr Whippy*.

But then he had chosen black. The blackest of black. Painted over each and every hesitant blue stripe until the bleak oily walls absorbed all colour and life.

She sees a man in paint-speckled navy overalls sidle up to the shelves of rollers and brushes. He is a grizzled grey—Barbed Wire Grey—and everything about him seems so tired: his folded-in eyelids, his not-so-erect lumbar spine, the creased, sad-sack clothes—and Fran wonders if being with a man like this would have made a scrap of difference for Damien, and whether her decision to not date men or pursue a relationship had been the right one after all. Pouring every ounce of her fibre and soul into her only son, as if growing a prize pumpkin for the Royal Show.

\* \* \*

The house smells horrible. Fran opens up all the windows and doors, and switches the air conditioner onto the fan setting. She examines the kitchen for signs of life then stands at Damien's door, pressing her ear lightly against the wood. Fran desperately wants to hear the sound of his breathing but all she can detect is her own irregular heartbeat. There is no light coming from under the doorway, only that constant flashing electric blue from the computer screen that Coral says *is as addictive as the pokies*. Oh yes, Coral has terrified Fran with stories about the Dark Web and the beastly, horror-show images that are traded and paraded for boys by the hour. What terrifies Fran the most is that she has no knowledge of the world which Damien now inhabits.

The doorbell rings and Fran is momentarily confused. She looks through the security screen and realises that she has forgotten the four o'clock appointment, the first client for her hastily set-up résumé-writing business. The contract with the private school will finish at the end of the year and she knows it won't be renewed. There have been far too many parent and student complaints for that.

'Have I got the right place?'

'Yes. Come in. I've got the office set up down here.'

The man follows Fran down the corridor. She feels uncomfortable letting a complete stranger into her home, but he looks innocuous enough. Ordinary features, office-style clothes and a polite, neutral voice. He has already sent through his details and qualifications, which Fran skimmed through last week. She vaguely remembers that he worked in a warehouse in Belmont and moved from Queensland six years ago. She apologises for not being organised and hurriedly prints out his documents while he waits patiently, taking in her office décor. Fran is quick, able to leap over the years and assess the situation. She likes this peephole into someone else's world, the ability to rearrange and embellish the small set of attributes and skills in order to compose a better, neater life. Align all those margins. Something bothers her though. Five missing years, and the man's dirty fingernails, which pick at a worn groove on his belt.

'Can you tell me what you were doing in 2009?'

'I just want a job.'

'I need a bit more information.'

'Can you do this or not?'

Fran wants to tell him that she cannot restore those lost years; the chinks in his timeline cannot be poly-filled with ink or bubbles of paint. She suddenly feels pity for him, apologises for not being able to help him after all. She gives a weak motherly smile.

'Are you fuckin' kidding me?' The man has the same look of incredulity on his face as Amy Hepple did when Fran dismissed her from her office, when she stared at the older woman and said, *Why are you even doing this job?*

Fran could not answer her. There was nothing to say. No-one ever grows up wanting to be a career guidance counsellor, or the mother of a son who cannot step one foot outside the front door.

\* \* \*

Fran doesn't go to sleep. She forces herself to stay awake just so she can get a glimpse of Damien and make sure he's okay. She takes a cup of coffee and waits in the lounge room at the front of the house with the light switched off. In the dull glow of the moon, she scrolls through the LinkedIn notifications on her phone. She's updated her profile but knows it won't make a difference. No-one will be headhunting her any time soon.

Sometimes she scrolls through the list of men called Simon Hobson. Or was it Hodson? It's been over twenty years since she woke up next to the stranger from the party, did the drive of shame down Kwinana Freeway, going against the peak-hour flow. She has forgotten everything about his face: it's hard to tell if it's Simon Hodson, a manager for Exxon, or Simon Hobson from Tech Solutions. She strains to find any trace of Damien in the suited necks and grainy faces.

In the stillness, Fran's heart is changing rhythm. On every fourth beat it feels as if it's a leg, kicking out all crooked, like a child learning how to swim. She can hear the puckered calls of the frogs coming from her garden fernery, how one low moan sets off the next, until the world is filled with the same stammering vibration of *love me, find me, love me, find me*. She wants to paper over the cries, just like she did when Damien screamed as a baby, smothering his wailing mouth with her nipple, force-feeding a gushing flow of milk down his gullet until he flopped like a drunk on her lap. The frog calls get stronger and more plaintive, and then she hears heavy footsteps down the hall. She stifles her breathing and switches off her phone. There is the sound of the fridge door unsticking its rubbery hold, and then dishes and jars being clanked around. The open door sets off a series of warning beeps and Fran knows that Damien is still standing there, shovelling the tray of lasagne into his mouth.

*A classic enabler.*

Fran hears him walk to the other end of the house; the toilet flushing and cistern gurgling. She is about to leave and go back to bed when suddenly she hears steps again and the click and slide of the glass doors opening. Where is Damien going? Curious, Fran creeps forward and sees a hulking creature standing like a statue in the garden. She watches in horror as Damien lifts up his blanket poncho and exposes his nakedness to the cool night air, his monstrous marbled belly hanging like an animal pouch over the tops of his white dimpled thighs, his penis a peeping worm. Then he turns his head to face her, and she's shocked to see he is now like an old man. The gloss of youth shrivelled away—wispy, thinning hair and dead eyes. *Click!* Fran steps forward to turn the lock, and Damien lets out a surprised bellow, screams and charges at his mother through the closed door. She watches all the rage and loathing, the hatred building to a climax on his face. And then she realises it's not Damien's reflection she can see, but her own: an angry, embittered middle-aged woman blinking unhappiness through the glass. For Damien is already running through the maze of unlit streets, his flesh wobbling in crazed momentum, his strange garment flapping like a dress and letting in the breeze.

# IN MEMORIAM

It was the night of the superstorm in Adelaide and I was sitting in the middle of Cousin Deidre's lounge room, surrounded by the remains of Walter's life. There were boxes of CDs and stationery, mementoes from the university and teaching years, science fiction paraphernalia, and of course the newspapers, decades of *The Advertiser* and *The Australian* bundled and stored to the height of the ceiling. I had made two circles in the midst of the mayhem, one for me and one for Cousin Deidre, and we had two small deckchairs set up as if we were on holiday at the seaside and not in this nightmare of a house.

Deidre is my cousin—not a first cousin, but some distant cousin on my father's side, and probably not a real cousin, even though for years it had been a matter of recourse to refer to her simply as Cousin Deidre. *Cousin Deidre is coming for Christmas*, or *Cousin Deidre has sent a postcard*. She was too young to be of my father's generation, but too old to be of mine, so she inhabited a generational space that was uniquely hers. For this reason, I never thought it odd that she wore childish overalls, or spoke in an affected voice that made her seem like she was born in Oxford rather than Clapham, South Australia. The only thing that jarred was her formalised use of the word 'mother' and not the friendlier moniker 'mum' that my friends and I had grown up with.

I was shocked at the state of her house, even though I had expected it. The last time I'd visited Adelaide was when Deidre's mother had died eight years ago, and I was summoned from the other side of the country to help sort out Aunt Gladys's small cottage—not because I was some organisational wizard, but because there was this assumption that I had the sort of life that is easily left.

Back then, Deidre's house was a bit of a shambles, though in a genteel, civilised way. There were books spilling out from the study alcove, and glass cabinets jam-packed with trinkets. Nonetheless, there was still a comfortable space for guests to sit on the sofas and place their teacups on side tables. But ever since Walter and his collections moved in, not long after Gladys's funeral, that all changed.

'We need a system,' I said, probably for the tenth time, as I knew from experience it was far easier to make plans than to execute them. 'Things to keep, things to give away and things to throw out.'

'I don't want to throw out too much,' said Deidre, with a frown.

'We can start with the obvious stuff. Like the newspapers.'

'There might be interesting articles. I would need to go through them first.'

I was stunned. It hadn't occurred to me that Cousin Deidre would be acting in this manner. When she had called my mum, who then called me, it was assumed that Walter's stuff had spiralled out of control and Deidre needed help with the clean-up. Was this a kind of Stockholm syndrome by proxy? Instead of falling in love with the captor, Deidre had fallen in love with his stuff.

'Okay,' I said, modulating my voice to make it sound less threatening. 'Let's at least sort out things for the Good Sammys. His clothes for starters.'

'I thought his friends might like those.'

'Okay—well, what's in the boxes over there?'

'His books. He had an excellent collection of fantasy and sci-fi.'

'You don't want to keep those?' I suggested hopefully.

'I thought of taking them to the funeral service. With the CDs, too. Setting up a trestle table in the church for his friends and family—as mementoes.'

'That's a good idea,' I said, even though I thought it sounded odd. 'So why don't we put these boxes straight into the car. That will clear more space in here, so you can use this room again.'

'But I need to go through them first. I thought about creating a bookshelf of his favourite books and CDs. Over there in the corner, as a memorial.'

Before I could even begin to think of an answer, the lamp behind me began to flicker weakly. Suddenly we were sitting in inky darkness, and I realised the rest of the lights in the place must have failed too. With all the concentration of the task at hand, I had simply blocked out the raging storm that had been battering the small house for the past few hours.

'The powerlines must be down. I've got some candles in the kitchen.'

'Use my phone,' I said, turning on its light and handing it over to Cousin Deidre.

I watched her weave her way slowly through the boxes and stacks of newspapers, like a mole wending its way through tunnels of its own making. When the electronic glow of the phone light finally disappeared, the darkness returned like a shroud. It felt weird sitting in a space that I didn't know, without the ability to make sense of it in my mind. Logic told me that the sensation of someone breathing down my neck was really the stack of newspapers towering behind me. It didn't help that Walter had died in this same house only three weeks earlier.

I could hear clattering and rattling noises, as Deidre searched the kitchen drawers for candles. Great sheets of rain pelted the windows and the wind whistled through the gaps in their frames. I remembered the suitcase I'd left out on the front doorstep because there'd been too many boxes in the entry hall to wheel it in. I had my university readings in there, plus my notebooks, and I hoped to God that the rain wasn't angling under the eaves and drenching my precious belongings. Whenever I pack to go somewhere, I take great delight in folding the best of everything in my life and seeing it arranged in neat squares in my suitcase: the newest underwear, the favourite jeans, the most expensive tops. All the crappy, regular stuff gets left behind.

'I've found them, Melanie!' I heard Deidre call out, and then her slow, torturous shuffle back to the lounge room. No doubt my cousin would be a whizz at solving those mazes in puzzle books.

She handed me my mobile, and I held our only source of illumination so she could strike the match and light the two candles.

'I think we should retire now and get up early,' Deidre said. 'I still need to sort out things for the service.'

'Good idea. The lights won't be going back on in a hurry.' I gripped my candle and followed her to the corridor. Even though there was enough light to see, I still rammed my knee into a sharp object that looked like a baby's pram from the Middle Ages.

Cousin Deidre stopped in front of an open doorway.

'This is where you'll be sleeping. I've cleared some space in the cupboard for your things. And I've made up the bed. It's Walter's room.'

Before I could protest, she disappeared through the opposite doorway. I inched my way into the room, placing my candle on the side table next to the bed. As I had nothing to get changed into, I stripped down to my knickers and crawled under the covers.

I thought about Walter. The fact that he had his own room intrigued me. I had assumed they were a couple. An odd one, mind you, both eccentric in their own way, and living seemingly disparate lives: Walter an introvert, who liked to stay close to the house, and Cousin Deidre always travelling on her own, using the money she had inherited from the sale of Gladys's cottage to fund her sojourns abroad. That's where she happened to be when Walter suddenly died of a heart attack, and why no-one had found him for ten days, until a concerned neighbour heard the dog howling and came over to investigate. How awful for Cousin Deidre to be told over the phone that her partner was dead, even worse to know that his body was left in this state for all that time. And then I had the terrible realisation that Walter could have died in this very bed, decomposing over those ten days, his bodily fluids seeping into the mattress as he evacuated faeces and urine in that final, mortifying dump. I felt the hysteria rising and hurriedly grabbed my mobile.

'Rache, it's me,' I said, when I heard her reluctant hello.

'Melanie. What's up?'

'It's terrible,' I whispered. 'I'm sleeping in Walter's bed. Where he probably decomposed...'

'What? I can't hear you.'

'I'm sleeping in Walter's room. He wasn't found for ten days. This place is a hovel—there's a storm outside and the lights are fucked and it's freakin' me out. I've got this creepy candle.'

All I could hear was Rachel's laughter swirling into my ear. She was laughing so hard she couldn't speak.

'I want to come home.'

'I thought you were staying for a week.'

'Why the hell did I agree to that? I've got too much to do—I'm so behind on everything.'

'Can you change your flight?'

'It's school holidays.'

'Any rats' nests, this time?'

That made me smile. Rachel had remembered that when I flew over to help with Gladys's cottage eight years ago, I had discovered a rats' nest in the laundry cupboard. And not just any ordinary rats' nest. One that had been lined with the shredded pages of *The Mill on the Floss*.

'Mel, I can't talk. I'm at work.'

'Oh... Okay. See ya.'

I tucked the phone under the edge of my pillow, and contemplated my choices. There was no other place to sleep, not even a usable sofa. So I decided to curl up, using the least amount of surface area on the bed I could. It was hard to relax. The wind whipped and shook the house, and there was a shattering noise as if someone was showering stones in the gutters.

I thought of Rachel. Even though we weren't together any more, she was my default person: the one to call whenever I was happy or sad. I pictured her brown, trusting eyes and the way she pushed her spiky fringe off her forehead with her signature yellow sweatband, making her look more like a tennis pro than a chef. Thinking of this made me forget about the condition of the mattress, and the wild, woolly storm battering the house, and the snuffling, scratching noises coming from beneath the bedroom door, and soon I drifted off into a deep sleep.

In the morning, it took me a few seconds to register where I was. And then I was leaping out of bed and pulling back the bottom sheet to check the state of the mattress. It looked brand spanking new. How weird. There was still the plastic protective cover on it, and the clinical smell of the furniture showroom. And that's when I realised that Walter's body must have been removed, bedding and all, straight to the morgue.

Rache would have a field day with this, I thought, as I got dressed and headed out to the living room. Cousin Deidre's golden labrador was whining at the back door, so I sidestepped all the junk to let it out. The backyard was a sea of weeds. There was still a sense of the formal English garden beds—arched rose trellises and flashes of colour where an iris or daffodil raised its delicate throat—but it wouldn't be too long before all sense of the borders would be lost.

I left the dog to plough heavily through the weeds and went into the kitchen to make a cuppa. This room was worse than I'd realised. The benches weren't just cluttered and overrun with crockery—the crockery was unwashed and all the surfaces were filthy. I rinsed out a cup and rummaged through the pantry for a box of tea. When I saw the stained, ancient Tetley Tea box, I decided against it and made my way back to the lounge room. I looked around at the task at hand and it seemed even more hopeless than the night before.

There was the sound of footsteps in the corridor and then Cousin Deidre poked her head over the top of the boxes. 'Good morning, Melanie. How did you sleep?'

'Fine.'

'Did Tuppence wake you? She used to sleep with Walter.'

'I think the storm woke me.'

'She's missing him terribly.' Deidre's face looked lopsided, squashed from her pillow.

'Cup of tea?'

'No, I'm okay,' I said a bit too quickly. 'I thought I'd get started on all the sorting.'

'Good idea. I was thinking last night about a display board for the service—a snapshot of all Walter's achievements.'

'Would we have time for that?' I asked doubtfully.

'It would be a shame for people not to see it.'

'So we should add another category then? Display board.'

'Yes. We'll call it the Wall of Achievement.'

# IN MEMORIAM

So that's what I did. I spent the entire day shifting the piles of Walter's life around the limited space in the living room while Deidre gave a running commentary. I would pick up a photo, or a lanyard, or a pamphlet and she would be off, filling me in on Walter's teaching days at the Catholic boys' school, his sudden retirement from the education system, and her serendipitous reconnection with him at the university reunion, weeks after her mother's death. It reminded me of when she and Aunt Gladys would come to visit us in Perth and set up their slide show in the outside storeroom, and Mum's and Dad's eyelids would grow heavy, seeing National Trust homes and ruined abbeys in places they had never heard of and would never visit, given their gruelling schedule at the newsagency. I wasn't interested in their travels either; instead, I marvelled at how Gladys's huge fleshy arms melted over the armrests of her chair as she barked out orders for Cousin Deidre to fix the height of the projector or switch the lights on and off.

And now it's Cousin Deidre, forearms swinging back and forth, telling me to *keep this photo*, and *put that book aside*, or *pin this to the Wall of Achievement*.

\* \* \*

At four o'clock, when all I had achieved were five burgeoning piles and no clearer floor space, Deidre announced that it was time to start working on the photos for the powerpoint presentation.

'Powerpoint,' I said incredulously. 'So that makes another category?'

'Yes, powerpoint. I thought it would be nice to have a selection of photos during the service—whilst they are playing the final hymn.'

'I'm not that great at powerpoint,' I muttered.

'Surely you do presentations at university?' she asked me, with a critical widening of one eye.

'Not really.'

'So, how is your dissertation going?'

And I answered as I did whenever my parents called me to ask. 'It's coming along nicely, thank you.'

It wasn't. I didn't have the courage to say that I was way behind schedule and my scholarship money had run out six months ago.

'What's it about, again?'

'Um, I'm arguing that David Malouf translates Gaston Bachelard's poetics of space into an Australian experience of house and home. How your childhood home corresponds to your psyche... The attic is the higher level, the basement the more primordial desires. Malouf uses this idea and flattens it into verandas and porches and the wide, open spaces of the Queenslander...' My voice dropped at the end, making me think I wasn't convinced either. What did I know about Queenslanders? I was brought up in a red-brick bungalow in Perth.

'That sounds interesting.'

'Have you got a computer I can use, Deidre?'

'Yes, but the power is still off. Hopefully there's enough battery life left in the old girl.'

I had forgotten about the power crisis. The storm had wiped out all the main power stations in South Australia and we were following the latest events via the small radio that Cousin Deidre had propped on her lap.

'It's somewhere in the study.' Deidre handed me the radio and did her two-step shuffle around boxes and disappeared.

All I wanted to do was go back to bed. Actually, on second thoughts, that would be the worse place to be. I surveyed the chaos around me. If Deidre cleaned up the place properly, the room would be quite liveable, even pretty. There were huge bay windows, floral chintz curtains (though in need of a good wash) and wooden floorboards that would polish beautifully to reveal their original oaken hues. In the same way Cousin Deidre would scrub up, too, if she had her hair trimmed, wore new clothes and lost a bit of weight.

I had thought the same about Walter the only time I'd met him, when they both flew over to Perth for Dad's sixtieth birthday. On first impression, he was a slovenly wreck, with an unironed shirt, shoulder-length greying hair, and a wobbling chin. He shyly stood back from the rest of the family, his hands hanging over his crotch as if hiding a secret, while Cousin Deidre spoke of their flight from Adelaide and made a big fuss over Dad. Walter only came alive when he confessed his love of the new Doctor Who episodes to me at dinner, and we had a momentary bonding over that, playfully arguing the merits of each Doctor. I could see in his face traces of the man Deidre had known and liked from university days.

When Deidre came back, I knew something was up. She had the same look Aunt Gladys always did when she inveigled someone into doing something for her.

'I forgot to tell you. My dear friend's husband is turning seventy tomorrow. I thought since you are a brilliant baker you could make the birthday cake.'

I felt my heart freeze over. Deidre continued, oblivious to my discomfort, 'I thought you could use Mother's famous fruit cake recipe and then decorate it in a golfing theme. Frank is an avid golfer.'

'I don't know if I'm the best person for the job,' I said.

'Of course you are! Remember your father's sixtieth birthday cake? It was splendid.'

I remembered that cake all right. It wasn't my cake at all. I had begged Rachel to make me a cake in the shape of Garfield, and I passed it off as my own, as Rachel was the little secret I was keeping from my family.

'Let me see if I can find Mother's recipe. The oven should work—it's gas.'

My mind was a blank and at the same time a crazy scribble of activity. I spent one moment staring at photos for the powerpoint, the next frantically trying to remember all the steps from when Rachel used to bake in our flat—cutting perfect strips of baking paper to line the tops of tins, scraping the sides of the bowl with a deft flip of the spatula. By the time the hands of the kitchen clock had inched around to 10pm, I had a basic powerpoint ready (though no decorative borders, no fade-in tricks) and a black-bottomed fruit cake cooling on the bench.

Luckily, Deidre was easily pleased. 'Wonderful,' she said, eyeing the wonky, singed cake on the wire rack. 'Now to bed! We have a busy morning tomorrow. We need to set up the church and finish icing the cake.'

I panicked all night about the damn cake. How the hell could I pull off a golfing theme? In the morning, the first thing I did was rummage in the pantry for anything that could be used for grass, for tees, for balls. I found green food colouring, a half-deflated bag of desiccated coconut and a single macadamia nut that must have rolled out of its bag some time ago and was stuck in the corner of the shelving. I smeared the cake with cup-loads of icing sugar mixed with the green food colouring, sprinkled on the green-drenched coconut for grass, made a 'Happy 70th Birthday' flag with a toothpick and coloured paper, and plonked the nut on top. It didn't look that bad. Quite good, in fact. I pulled out my phone, took a photo and sent it to Rachel, then raced to get all the boxes out the front door, ready for my lift to the church. The power was still off, and Cousin Deidre's car was stuck in the garage behind the electric roller door, so she had organised another distant relative, Cousin Gordon, to pick me up. When he stood at the front door and saw the mess, I thought his eyes were going to detach themselves from their sockets. We struggled back and forth, carrying all the boxes to his Toyota, and loading them into the boot and over the seats. Then we took off, leaving Cousin Deidre behind in her flannelette nightie to start work on the eulogy.

It's hard talking to a distant cousin when you have no idea how you are related. Cousin Deidre had previously tried explaining it to me, but my eyes glazed over and my brain switched off when she showed me the family tree on a tablecloth-sized ream of paper. More branches than the varicose veins in Gladys's calves.

The superstorm was a good out. That took up a lot of car time, as I let him talk about the failed Labor policy and how closing down all the coal-fired power stations was too short-sighted. 'The Libs would never have let this happen,' he sighed. What could I say to that? I had no interest in politics. Rachel was always saying that I should spend more time reading about the news and less with my nose in a novel.

Gordon must have sensed my lack of interest, for he changed tack. 'Terrible about Walter,' he said. 'Ironic though. How he died in bed reading the paper.'

Normally irony is something that would excite me, but I couldn't get beyond the words 'in bed'.

'I think Deidre's feeling a little guilty, for not being there when it happened,' he continued. 'But when your time's up, your time's up.'

'He wasn't that old, was he?' I asked.

'Same age as Deidre. He really hit the jackpot when he moved in with her.' I detected a faint note of disapproval and wondered if this critical tendency was an inherited trait. I hoped the turkey neck wasn't.

We pulled up at the church, a beautiful building, just like all the other churches we had passed in Adelaide, with golden, hallowed stonework and an iron steeple. We unloaded the car and I followed Gordon, with the first of my many boxes, to set up. Gordon stopped at a marble plaque in the entrance and in a reverent, hushed tone said, 'This is William's memorial stone—our ancestor. He helped build this church.' I murmured recognition and made a note to myself to locate a William on the family tree—that was obviously the nexus point of all these distant cousins.

Inside, there were three elderly ladies setting up the trestle tables for the afternoon tea.

'Did you bring the flowers?' one of them asked.

'No. What flowers?'

'Deidre was bringing flowers for the tables. Didn't she tell you?'

'She must have forgotten. She mentioned something about display boards?'

'Yes, they're in the Sunday school room. And you can also use those spare trestle tables.'

So Gordon and I set to work rolling in the boards from the other room, and getting the books and CDs out of their boxes and arranging them methodically. A table for sci-fi, a table for non-fiction, a table for CDs from the eighties and one for the nineties. Then we moved onto the display boards, dividing these into his uni years, teaching years, sci-fi conferences and his casual job at the cricket ground. I stood back from the boards and noticed there were big, unaccounted gaps in Walter's life.

'Are we missing a box?' I said to Gordon, a bit worried.

'That looks about right. Unless it's still in storage.'

'Storage?'

'Didn't you know? Walter had a storage unit he kept his stuff in. Of course, Deidre was paying for that, too.'

'I didn't know.'

It was too late to try and find the relevant boxes. Anyway, Walter was dead and people would be too grief-stricken to notice a dodgy timeline. I glanced at the clock on the wall and panicked. I had only thirty minutes to get back to Cousin Deidre's place, get changed and then come back in time for the service. As we were leaving for the car, one of the kitchen ladies called out, 'Don't forget the flowers!'

\* \* \*

As soon as I walked into the house I knew that same sense of urgency wasn't present. There was classical music playing, the sound of the stovetop kettle whistling in the kitchen and Cousin Deidre still noodling around in her slippers and nightie.

'Deidre. It's time to leave. We only have five minutes.'

'Oh, but I haven't had a shower yet.'

'Jump in now!' I couldn't believe how assertive I was being.

I ran to my suitcase and flung it open to find the only dress I had packed. I'm not usually a dress person, but this one I had bought at the Fremantle Markets with Rachel. It was a retro black and green dress with a huge collar and a tightly fitted belt that Rachel said made me look like that actress from the show *Mad Men*.

I remembered the flowers. 'Deidre,' I called through the bathroom door. 'Are we supposed to be picking up flowers?'

'You need to pick them from the garden.'

Gordon was standing in the hallway ready to go. I handed him my handbag and ran outside into the backyard and through the mud and dog shit. I aimed for the heads of bobbing colour amongst the weeds. A blue iris, a yellow daffodil. Soon I had a decent armful of flowers and brought them inside.

I was brutal. 'DEIDRE, INTO THE CAR NOW!'

When we arrived at the church, we could hear the piped sounds of the organ playing. I told Deidre to go ahead while Gordon and I took the flowers into the kitchen.

'Sorry we're late,' I said to the three ladies, who were busy cutting the crusts off sandwiches and checking the water level in the urn. 'Do you have any vases I can use?'

'Leave that with us, luv. You'd better get to the service.'

'Aren't these ladies lovely,' I whispered to Gordon on the way out.

'They should be, at thirty dollars an hour.'

The first thing I observed when we walked down the aisle was how empty the chapel appeared. There was a family group sitting in the front pew, Deidre directly behind them, and a small smattering of people spaced out like single pegs through the rest of the church. I sat next to Deidre, and I could see straightaway that she was nervous, and focusing on re-reading the eulogy silently to herself. I patted her hand. She looked really nice, with her black slacks and a fuchsia silk top that I had never seen before. And I could see that she was also wearing Gladys's old screw-on earrings, little diamanté flowers clamped like small vices to her fleshy lobes.

The first person to speak was Walter's aunt and it didn't augur well, for she started with the words, 'Walter was an odd child.'

The next speaker wasn't any better. An old school friend who finished with the line, 'And now when the phone doesn't ring bang on dinner time, my wife and I will strangely miss Walt.'

And then a former teaching colleague saying, 'Walter was the most brilliant man I knew. With an eidetic memory, who could move from the fall of the Roman Empire to string theory in a single breath. Until his nervous breakdown. Such a waste.'

People looked uncomfortable; some stared at their programs. I studied my hands, which still had a hue of turf green. And then it was Deidre's turn, and she made her way slowly to the lectern, eyes trained on her feet as if she was worried about stumbling. She took out a pair of spectacles, cleared her throat and began.

She spoke of how she had first met Walter at university, where they connected as shy teenagers sharing a love of history and reading. And how they had lost touch since graduation, only reconnecting years later at the reunion, where she was shocked to see that he had holes in his shoes and that he had been living on the streets. They were peas in a pod. Both only children, brought up in poverty by strong single mothers who instilled in them a thirst to better themselves through education. Yes, life had been a struggle for Walter, but the last eight years had been good to him. He had thrived with her. Had a home, the means to buy clothes, books, and go to concerts and sci-fi conferences. He was excited about his quest to finally write his life's opus; hence, all the research articles and newspapers he couldn't bear to part with. She finished with the words, 'He was my soul mate and I was the happiest I have ever been in my life.' The tears flowed down her face. Then the powerpoint started, and there were the photos of a baby on a sheepskin rug, the boy on a bike, smiles at graduation, and a picture of Walter holding court under the shade of a eucalyptus tree, with a circle of earnest-looking boys in uniform. The final shot was the same photo printed on the funeral service booklet: Walter in front of Deidre's house, collecting the newspaper from the front lawn with a goofy smile illuminating his entire face.

There was a minute's silence after it finished, as people studied the photo in their programs as if discovering for the first time the pixelated meanings in that smile, that newspaper.

After the service, everyone trickled into the kitchen area for the afternoon tea and to view the trestle tables. It took on the feel of a garage sale: people rummaging through for a bargain, picking up five items and hugging them under their armpits. I noticed a few men gathered around the Wall of Achievement, and I was pleased—until I realised they were only scanning the boards for things relating to themselves. When I saw the kitchen ladies walk across and begin to rifle through the CDs I wanted to explode. But then my eyes caught sight of Deidre standing at the periphery, and she was looking at everything with a serene, beatific smile.

'It was a lovely service,' I said to her gently.

'I wish he could have seen all of this.'

'Deidre,' I began slowly. 'I have to go back to Perth on Sunday to sort out my own life, but I'll be back later to help you with the storage unit. And I thought I'd bring a friend. She's kind of *my* soul mate... I think you would like her.'

'That would be perfect,' Deidre said, smiling not at me, but at Walter's towering wall.

# GODDESS OF FIRE AND WIND

It was supposed to be the trip of a lifetime. The honeymoon they never had—seeing parts of the world Margaret had only ever dreamed of. But it was nothing like she had imagined, for her husband would not stop at the market stalls on the side of the road or veer off to leisurely follow the signs advertising farmhouse devonshire teas. Like the true engineer he was, everything was scheduled and broken down into ratios of time versus money versus maximum satisfaction. And now at their final destination of Hawaii before they returned home to Australia, when all she wanted was to feel the warm sands of Waikiki Beach between her toes and drink sunset-coloured Mai Tais, they were stuck in budget accommodation on the Big Island just so Des could see an active volcano and tick that off his spreadsheet.

The trek over the fields of lava was to begin at 5pm, a private tour run by a local guy named John, which Des had found on a travel forum and was touted as an experience like no other. Des entered the destination into the GPS, and they set off thinking they had plenty of time to get there, but they hadn't factored in the winding roads, the extra caution in driving on the right-hand side of the road or the long queue of cars at a standstill on Kaimu-Chain of Craters Road.

'Oh, great,' Des muttered. 'John specifically said not to be late.'

'Are you sure this is the right road? It looks like people are being stopped.'

'Of course it's the right road. I'm following the map exactly.'

'But are we allowed to be here? Look! They're turning everyone away.'

Margaret could see men dressed in security uniforms walk alongside each car and bend their heads into the windows to have a word with the drivers, and then the vehicle would pull out of the queue and do a U-turn at the roadblock set up at the end of the street. It must have been going on for some time, for a bored-looking woman, dressed in sweatpants with a long grey ponytail and cap set backwards, sat at a home-made booth selling water bottles and flashlights.

Soon it was their turn. The security guy came over, and Des wound down his window.

'Where you headed, folks?'

Des bared his teeth—his attempt at a smile—and retrieved the printed-out email stashed in the middle console that gave John's address. The uniformed man glanced at the paper, and for a moment Margaret thought they, too, would be turned away. But the man nodded and waved them on through a side gate onto a private road which wound up to the scattered homes built directly on the old fields of lava.

'See. I told you so,' Des said, smugly.

It was a scene of devastation and hope. The ground—blackened, twisted runnels and furrows with a strange assortment of dwellings built on top, like defiant castles. Some had attempted to create gardens—raised vegetable beds and grown scarlet-flamed plants in pots—but it was the houses with nothing but black glistening yards that had the greatest visual impact.

'This must be the place.' Des stopped the car in front of the two-storey home on stilts with an expansive viewing deck.

'This is incredible,' Margaret said, imagining a life sitting on that deck.

'Bloody stupid. It's like living on the side of Mount Vesuvius.'

At that moment another car pulled in behind them, and they glanced at each other, only now realising that their private, expensive tour included other people. They grabbed the camera and lightweight backpacks and made their way to the front door.

Before they could knock, a rangy man stepped out to greet them. 'John,' he said, shaking their hands and staring at their footwear, not bothering to make eye contact.

'Good. Everyone's on time. We need to get started before sunset.'

'Can I use the bathroom?' Margaret asked, suddenly doubting the strength of her bladder.

John appeared surprised by her request, as if no-one had asked this before. He took her inside and showed her the bathroom. Margaret tried to hurry, but her bladder wasn't full. She needed to push out a few drops of urine so she wouldn't be bothered by a feeling of incompleteness. It gave her time to take in all the details of the bathroom: the rustic wooden sink bench, a blue and yellow mosaic dolphin mirror, and a mural of a Hawaiian woman with heavy breasts and a flowering vagina—literally, a flower! A red, moist, petalled organ, which waved to her like a giant hand.

Maybe this was what John didn't want her to see. Or the curlicues of black hair stuck along the grouting at the edge of the wall, or the strong stink of male urine. Though, walking back to the front door, her eyes took in enough of the living room décor to determine that a woman had moved her hand over this place once.

'Your house is amazing,' Margaret said, as a way to reconnect with the quiet group waiting outside.

'It's a difficult life. Not many people can last.'

'Because you're so close to the lava flows?' Des asked.

'No, it's the wind. Some people go crazy with the sound of the wind.'

'I can't believe you'd want to take the risk. Wasn't this housing estate wiped out not long ago?' Des said, stuck on his own line of thinking, and John nodded without much conviction. He looked like he had heard this all before.

'The land is dirt cheap. Where else can you afford a view like this?'

Margaret could see their eyes had only focused on the bleak fields of black, for there on the horizon was the bluest jewel of sea.

'Awesome. We could definitely live here. Couldn't we, Phoebes?' The man who said this was in his twenties and had an American accent. He was diminutive and open faced; his female partner was on the short side too, with a clamped-up, surly expression.

'I have walking sticks for those who need them. Remember the lava is like glass; if you fall you'll be cut to pieces. And watch where you're walking—I had a guy who got wedged in a crevice and snapped his ankle. Here are some head torches for when it gets dark.' John passed out the torches to the group, and Margaret noticed that she was the only one who took up the offer of a stick. 'We'll be going through private land until we get to the stretch along the coast. Try and keep up with me. We've only got four hours.'

That worried her. The idea of being on a tight schedule and the condition of her knees. The younger people would be fine, and her husband's doggedness would see him through, but she worried that she would be the factor slowing them all down. John started at a cracking pace, but the rest of them were more tentative, trying to work out how to negotiate the uneven, unknown terrain, and not letting their eyes leave the ground. They passed a single banana chair left out for sunbaking, and only when she heard the American guy say, 'Awesome,' did she turn to see that it had been trapped in a solidified previous flow.

It troubled Margaret seeing it stuck like that. It reminded her of when she was a young woman, before she was married, and she went to see the touring Pompeii AD 79 exhibition in Perth. There were ancient artefacts, jewellery, pieces of broken pottery, cooking utensils, but the glass display that everyone was drawn to was the plaster casts of the lovers entwined on the ground, frozen in their death throes.

'Try to keep up,' shouted John, who was metres ahead. And Margaret realised that she was falling further behind the others, who had now stepped up their momentum. She levered her walking stick against the hard furrows to help herself move faster. She could see that the younger man, Tyler, had caught up to John by now and was easily matching the guide's long-legged strides. Des was not far behind the two men, but she could imagine the strain of exertion for him just to keep up. Occasionally she would try and guess the distance covered, and allow herself to see something extraordinary, like a small sapling bowing in the breeze, its roots anchored in the crevices. The rest of the time, it was nose to the ground and desperately trying not to fall.

She'd been so focused on her own footsteps that she only now noticed she had drawn parallel to the young woman—Phoebe, wasn't it?—who puffed and cursed under her breath, and moved in such a cumbersome way it seemed as if she would tumble over. Margaret could see that their pacing was now completely in sync. Unless one of them changed their stride, they would be walking side by side the entire time. There was no choice but to make small talk.

'Where are you from?'

'San Francisco.'

'Oh, on the San Andreas fault line.'

'Yeah. I guess.'

'I'm from Perth—Western Australia. Even Perth isn't that safe. There was an earthquake in the sixties in a country town called Meckering. I remember we even felt the shock waves all the way in Cannington—we had this enormous crack in our driveway.'

How stupid she was sounding. Stupid, stupid! She had done the same thing on their leg to New Zealand. At The Living Maori Village in Rotorua, as her husband took photos of the Maori woman lifting up the basket of sweet potato cooked in the steaming springs, she told the tour guide standing next to her that being in Rotorua made her feel on edge. Like she was living on the top of a kettle.

'I'm Margaret,' she offered now, but the young woman pretended not to hear.

The humiliation was burning on her cheeks so she tried to edge away from Phoebe, but not so fast as to give away her true feelings. She watched the blackness twist at her feet—crow-coloured, and mangled, like train tracks from a wreck—knowing that each and every footfall mattered, and if she stopped to look ahead or behind, Phoebe would catch up.

The light was fading from the sky, and she couldn't help but lift her head and see that she was now nearing the cliffs, and gaining ground on the three dark figures in the distance. And then she realised that they hadn't stopped to wait for their partners, but because they had reached their final destination. She turned to Phoebe. 'Almost there,' she called out.

Margaret felt the tension build to a heaviness in her legs and a pain beginning to radiate from her kneecap. And then, all of a sudden, there was a shocking cracking sound, and she looked to her knee, to her foot, to the ground, to see that the tip of her stick had snapped. Now her stick was a useless twig that she wanted to throw away but had to keep, so she could explain the loss to John. Not knowing what else to do, she lifted it up and used it to keep her balance, as a tightrope walker does.

As she inched closer to the men, they began yelling instructions at her. It frightened Margaret not knowing what they were saying. She stopped to listen and felt a heat pounding beneath her shoes, but when she examined the ground it looked no different to the land she had already crossed.

Des walked towards her, and now she could make out his words, 'Can you feel it? We're right on top of the flow.' How strange. She never expected this: the lava hidden beneath her feet. 'How are your knees holding up?'

'Perfectly fine,' she answered coolly.

Phoebe caught up to them and then walked past, muttering and stumbling and fighting with her backpack, and Des said, 'God, what's up with her?'

They followed Phoebe, and soon all of them were reunited on the edge of the cliff.

'Not long to go now, and you'll see the full force of Pele,' said John.

'Isn't the volcano called Kīlauea?' Margaret asked.

'Pele—the goddess of fire and wind. And the creator of all the islands.'

'Cool,' said Tyler, rubbing Phoebe's neck.

'It's her energy that attracts people here in the first place. If she doesn't want you to stay, you'll soon know about it.'

'How long have you been living here?' Margaret asked John.

'Since 2007,' he answered.

She wanted to ask, 'But why did *she* leave?' when Tyler called out, 'Awesome!' They looked to where he was pointing and saw trails of glowing red coming from the volcano in the distance. Now that it was dark enough, they could see what had always been there.

'Take a look at the water,' John said, and they looked down at the ocean, where the waves smashed against the rocks, and great sparks of fire cascaded over the cliff. And, as if a switch had been turned on, three boats suddenly appeared around the island's bend, a helicopter swooped in like a dragonfly above them, and teams of sightseers, led by their guides, crossed the lava fields from the opposite direction.

'So much for the private tour,' muttered Des, lowering his camera.

It didn't bother her, not to be alone. She looked down at the lava pouring into the ocean and the coconut palms growing at jaunty angles along the emerging coastline, and thought, this is how the world begins.

For minutes no-one spoke. They were all taking in this spectacle of heat and fire and hissing ocean, letting the red rivers of lava glow on their retinas. A camera lens could never capture it; the retelling of it in an email to your adult children would never do it justice.

'Can we get to see the lava close up?' asked Tyler.

John nodded and indicated they switch on their torches and follow him. The group walked further inland until John held up his hand. Coming through a tube in the ground was a lava flow, moving like a slow, fat slug.

'Awesome!' And Tyler plunged his hand into his backpack, whipping out a bag of marshmallows and a long toasting fork.

'You won't be able to bear the heat,' warned John.

'I saw this on YouTube.'

Tyler put on a silver-foiled glove and bent over the fat finger of lava, a marshmallow on each fork prong. After a few seconds, he checked to see if they had caramelised enough, and offered one to Phoebe.

'You know I don't eat sugar,' she snapped.

'Sorry, babe. Anyone else want one?'

'Sure.' Des stepped forward and took the marshmallow, then popped it in his mouth.

'You should try one,' he said to Margaret.

'I was going to,' she hissed at him.

'How was I supposed to know? I'm not a bloody mind-reader.'

Margaret flinched and moved towards John. 'I didn't realise it moved so slowly. You'd have plenty of warning to leave, if it came too close.'

'During the last close shave, we had enough time to load our stuff in the car and throw a party on the front deck. It's all out of our hands though. It's up to Pele, whether we stay or go.'

She couldn't see John's face in the dark, but his voice gave away an insincerity, as if he had given up on Pele some time ago.

'We'll have to head back,' John said, checking his watch. 'It takes longer in the dark.'

Margaret no longer cared if she slowed them down. They had seen what they needed to, and John had already been paid a tremendous amount of money. What did an extra hour mean to anyone?

On the way back, Des stayed closer to her, just as Tyler did with Phoebe. The dark seemed to bring out the protective quality in the men. And walking back was, surprisingly, easier. Her eyes were made to home in on the small prick of light emanating from her torch, a circle of trust that seemed to give her more assurance than daylight ever could. The kind of comfort given to their ancestors as they huddled around a campfire while the mountains and valleys crashed and moved all around them.

Margaret could sense a change in her husband now, and she knew that when they got back to the hotel he would go to the bathroom and use the mouth gargle, always the sure sign he would be expecting sex that night. She would have to muster up a vestige of desire, something which was becoming harder and harder these days. She thought about the cheap room they were staying in, decked out in the dated décor: the pine panelling on the walls and the bedspread with the pastel pink seashells. There were no fluffy his and hers matching bathrobes, the kind that Bob Hawke and Blanche were photographed in on the cover of the *Woman's Day* all those years ago. There was no bath-tub, just a shower with an unsatisfying nozzle that dribbled water out from the sides. Still, she would take her time in the bathroom and make Des wait. And if he was still awake when she finally emerged, steaming and all clean, she would make him slow down and take his time, so that when she felt the prickle of heat in her groin building to an unbearable crescendo, it would be allowed to build and build until it had nowhere else to go.

# WARM BODIES

Hugh knew within minutes of meeting the young British engineer at the airport that he would have to shake him off. Even a little shared experience was enough to bind you to someone unnaturally. The two men had arrived in Guinea at the same time and were now making their way with their driver through Conakry's littered streets and seeing the detritus of the shanty towns: layers of rotting cardboard and rusted corrugated sheets under which humans cooked, urinated, slept. Then driving into open countryside and being amazed by the yawning blue African skies—more of a revelation to Matt, for Hugh was used to the Western Australian outback. But what was really surprising were the villages: the rows of mud huts and orderly pens for livestock, the plentiful supply of chickens, cattle, clean air, and no filth clogging the ruts in the roads or stuck like papier-mâché on city kerbsides.

Why would you ever leave your villages, Hugh wondered, watching the children, free-range and delirious, become black-limbed hieroglyphics—jerky in the distance, as their truck drove further inland and away from the coast. To leave this for what? The silent pull of a collapsible city, piling onto the existing stratum layers of rubbish, metal sheets and humans; hand to tin, soiled cardboard to limb, with what manner of diseases incubating in that slag heap. Gonorrhoea, dysentery, cholera... all utterly curable; however, here in Guinea the rules of living were so different.

And then, driving into the dusky mauve nightfall, where the bruised sky merged almost indiscernibly into the shadowy mountain ranges, and there at the base campsite, a legoland of small rectangles in a cleared space.

'Holy shit,' said Matt. Hugh wondered if he was referring to the orange dongas that were really old sea containers, or the six black guards standing at the boom gate nursing their rifles.

They were relieved to find they were staying not in the sea containers but in the newer part of the compound, in dongas built by the company's Chinese co-venture partners, though a deceptive gift. *Made by the Origami Masters in China*, the other men joked, walls so paper thin you could hear every bowel movement, every cough in the building next door, and each time you showered, the plastic floors of the shower cubicles cracked and split so that small rivulets of effluent seeped over your toes.

Matt's room was next to Hugh's, so if you removed the thin partition their beds would lie side by side like they were having a permanent sleepover. Sometimes Matt would knock on the wall and try to talk, and Hugh would lie still, pretending to be fast asleep. Hugh could see the younger man was desperate to build on the friendship. Each meal break he brought his tray to Hugh's table, and shadowed him in the downtimes. He was a young man in his late twenties, with a healthy flush to his face, a surface flow of capillary blood in his cheeks that made him come across as immature and without any substance. An eagerness to please like a puppy, something which bothered Hugh and he felt mean in thinking so. On the fourth morning, when Matt walked over to the table, laden with a tray full of food, Hugh quickly hunched over his smartphone, shut him down with that one closed-off gesture, so that Matt blushed then joined the Australians laughing at the other table.

Hugh settled for the South Africans instead. Afrikaners. He had worked with Afrikaners all through the Pilbara and preferred their looming, almost taciturn presence, and solid proletariat hands that had so easily shifted from farming to mining over several generations. An unspoken yet implied arrogance—the knowledge that they were Afrikaner seemed to be enough—which suited Hugh because that was how he saw himself. It wasn't that he wasn't good around people; he could be personable if he wanted. Hugh's self-containment came from knowing that he had already found his place in the world, a tight nucleus that was the certainty of family—his wife Kate and their three children. Ever since he met his wife at university, she had become his best friend, and whether he orchestrated it or she did, their need for others slowly diminished. Over the years their world had grown smaller, probably the legacy of living in a succession of mining towns and moving on before any real attachments formed, any roots grew. That didn't mean Kate wasn't good with others either. He marvelled at the way she could fast-track intimacies each time they moved from town to town, becoming an indispensable friend to some poor woman who couldn't cope with the searing heat or not having a Westfield shopping centre up the road. Dropping off lasagnes, organising play dates for the kids, and then the minute the Centurion van pulled up and the boxes were packed and stacked Kate would forget them. Sincerely insincere or insincerely sincere? It didn't matter because each night there she was, her body warm beside his and a child between them with a leg or arm flung out, treating both parents as a silent mooring.

* * *

He had broken their marriage vow to come to West Africa. A promise to Kate that no matter what, he would never do fly in, fly out work and leave the family behind. But he hadn't factored in being seduced by the story of the mountain, or Carston's retelling of it—and, really, it all came to the same thing.

Hugh had met the retired exploration geologist months ago in the Perth office, and he sensed straightaway that 'old school' knowledge, the breadth of experience that spanned more than one continent, more than one lifetime. Carston was grey and stooped, yet with a flinty focus that sharpened him, taking years off him, though his quavering voice was the giveaway. He stood in front of the tenth-storey window, and the light glittered and refracted from the other skyscrapers and the cranes which crisscrossed the skyline, illuminating this life of uncharted estuaries and unmapped riverbeds, lighting the wiry body from within the pale checked shirt, and Hugh realised this was exactly the life he wanted.

'We first heard about the legend of the iron mountain from the French,' Carston explained, sounding more like a storyteller than a geologist, and clearly relishing the opportunity to hold centre stage. 'The French discovered the mountain during an earlier expedition through West Africa—estimated it to be about a billion tonnes of continuous mineral. So when we explored the area in the seventies, we took a team of pack bearers and headed out there ourselves. I'll never forget that moment when we arrived at the mountain...' Carston paused, as if for effect, his penetrating eyes, brilliant beacons of light. 'The mountain was completely veiled by thick, dense cloud, and as we walked through it, the mist suddenly lifted and there it was: miles and miles of blue haematite, breaking through the alluvial layers. The French had got their estimates completely wrong—more iron than we ever could have dreamed of.'

Everyone in the office had a good laugh over that one: laughed at the bloody French; had a chuckle over the fact that no other company had sought to mine the mountain of iron ever since.

And now as Hugh tried retelling this story to the Afrikaner superintendent driving the truck as they travelled towards the forest-covered ranges, it came across with the flatness of an anecdote. Hugh could not channel the essence of Carston, and Gerhard had already seen the mountain. The punchline was a given. Matt sat behind Hugh, and he could feel the young man's hot breath as an irritant on his neck.

'Why the hell didn't the French mine it years ago?' asked Matt.

'Sovereign risk. That's why we have the Chinese on board. The Guinean government wouldn't dare fuck with the Chinese.'

Hugh sat in silence. He couldn't be bothered talking any more, his eyes now set on the mountain ahead. He could see what Carston had meant. Even from this distance you could see the intense blue where there were patches of missing vegetation from landslides, like the colour of arteries on an anatomy chart when the skin is peeled away. The truck churned into a lower gear where the road became steep and narrow, and then Gerhard stopped the vehicle saying, 'From now on, we walk.' A ute pulled up behind them, and three armed guards jumped off the back.

'Bit of overkill,' muttered Matt.

'Not when a leopard's ripping off your face,' answered Gerhard.

The small group walked slowly up the mountain, with Gerhard explaining the future mining plans to Matt who took photos as they walked on ahead, and Hugh stopping every few metres or so to gather some soil samples. The African guards lingered behind, watching him with interest as he picked up the sand and let it run like mini waterfalls through his hands. Hugh looked around. He couldn't believe what he was seeing, the scale of the mountain and what it potentially was worth to the company. He had only been involved with projects at the middle or end of their life. Like Mount Tom Price, a small mining town in the Pilbara, though by the time he had arrived it was known only as Tom Price. The whole mountain had already been carted away in the ore trains that snaked their way to the coast.

Hugh noticed that the others had stopped abruptly, and were focused on the shadows thrown from the giant trees twisting up from a gully. The trail had been an easy walk through light scrub, making it obvious to see what lay metres ahead. But down in the undulations of valley and ravine—as if a giant had pressed its thumbs into primordial dough—there grew a dense, impassable forest. It was strangely quiet, no bird or animal life could be heard, but Hugh's eyes were drawn to the movement on the ground.

Matt whispered, 'Can you see it?'

Hugh strained his eyes, not quite getting what he was seeing. He could make out the chimpanzee hunched over watching them, but it was the thing on its back that confused him. It was flat and insubstantial, like a dried-out husk, with two long dangly legs unnaturally stretched out like a spider's.

'Poor bugger doesn't know it's dead,' said Matt.

Shit. A mummified infant. Hugh watched as the mother chimp turned to move away, and then he could make sense of the baby, how it was really just black wizened skin, with those elongated limbs stuck to the length of its mother's back. One of the guards lifted his gun as if to shoot the poor creature, and Gerhard shouted out something hard and guttural, and the chimp took fright, limbering into the forest and away from sight.

Hugh was shocked. 'Aren't they endangered? Should he be doing that?'

And Gerhard responded coolly, 'What do you think the "special meat" advertised in the villages is?'

\* \* \*

When Hugh skyped his wife that night and tried to tell her the story—horror for the spidery legs, sorrow for the mother—it was lost in the two-second delay. He noticed that Kate had developed a strange diffidence over the screen, probably because they weren't used to gazing directly at each other: sitting side by side, feeding the children, watching television on the sofa, but never opposite like this. He could see she was embarrassed, then she jiggled the computer away from her face and he saw flashes of wall, skirting board as she moved to the children's bedrooms, zooming in on their sleeping faces—a fringe of dark lash, a soft doughy arm flopped over a teddy. He felt the pain of not being there, of not breathing in their skin.

'When are you coming home?' he heard Kate say, her face off-centre and forehead looming larger at this angle.

'Three weeks, max.'

There was a pause, or was it the natural delay, and then she said, 'Love ya,' and he replied without hesitation, 'Love ya, too.' So easy to say; their trademark words exchanged in such a nonchalant, throwaway manner, and with the same tone his own mother would invoke when he looked a little melancholic as a boy and she would invariably say, *Chin up*.

He should have explained to Kate that there was a certain rhythm of life in West Africa, how what would normally be a one-week job stretches out to a month. How in the mess it takes five women to scrape the plates clean; at the building site, six men to watch one man work the jackhammer. And it wasn't that the locals were lazy. Hugh had seen enough of slackers on projects over the years to call them out. No, it was something different, maybe the pace of village life where a frenzy of activity like hunting or farming preceded a quiet time of mulling over the significance of the kill and the crop. And for years the locals had been promised the bounty of the iron mountain and still the project was in the evaluation phase and nothing had eventuated, being stopped by one obstacle or another: a change of government, or a massive plummet in the ore prices. Or maybe they were just pacing themselves, taking one long, deep breath before things really got started.

Hugh looked at the clock by his bed. He wasn't tired but if he didn't sleep now he would be struggling to wake in time for breakfast with the team in the mess. He could imagine Kate padding across the kitchen lino and brewing her first cup of coffee before the kids woke for school, lining up squares of white bread across the sink to defrost for school lunches. They would share the coffee in the pot, talk about the children and the other women in the town, and then one child would awake, and, like a noisy domino effect, suddenly it would be mayhem, screams and laughter and little arms lifted in the air to be dressed and then the hot, cross shouts from his youngest daughter as Kate tried to tame the frizzy scarecrow hair into two pigtail bushels.

There was that familiar pang across his chest as he remembered all of this, and then it was subdued as quickly as it had come.

* * *

The latest delay was the matter of the chimpanzees. Hugh was at the meeting in the superintendent's office when the environmental officer delivered the grim news.

'A colony of chimps to the east of the mine. It will be tricky getting approval.'

The Chinese manager's face was a death mask. A man in his thirties with skin as smooth as a woman's, not a single blemish or wrinkle to mar his oval face.

'Get it sorted.'

'Shouldn't be a problem,' answered Gerhard. 'We have the animals' interests more at heart than the locals do.'

And that was probably true. Hugh hadn't told anyone about the previous day, when he had gone into the cafeteria and the food was the usual inedible, unrecognisable slop, except for the fish heads bobbing in an oil-slick stew.

'I'd like to know what happened to the rest of the fish,' joked the Australian guy ahead of him in the line.

Hugh decided to skip the stew and piled a mound of the green vegetable onto his plate instead. *Kava*, he thought the young woman standing at the bain-marie had said when he asked her what it was. He must have heard incorrectly. It looked like silverbeet and tasted of the earth. He had seen it growing everywhere in the fields, seeded behind the sheds and in the gullies, and there was always a constant haze of smoke as the villagers cleared more land for the ubiquitous crop.

The slippery, slimy vegetable barely made a dent in his appetite, and Hugh left the cafeteria hungry. A startling aroma drifted across the compound, assailed his senses and he found himself following the smell to where two black women were standing at a large iron cauldron, smoky tendrils enveloping their bare arms and shiny, generous faces.

A group of men sat on benches under a tarpaulin and Hugh could see that this was the cafeteria designated for the unskilled labour force. The women were animated, unlike those serious young girls who worked in the main mess hall, and when they saw him, they stopped their chatter and lowered their eyes.

'Smells great,' said Hugh, peering into their pots and seeing a bubbling meat stew.

The older woman burst into laughter, couldn't contain her grin. 'Would you like to try?'

Hugh hesitated, sensing a joke, but the hunger gnawing at his belly had become untenable and he nodded. 'Why not?'

Her strong arms stirred the pot, scraping the tastier, fried bits caught at the cast-iron bottom. She lifted the heavy ladle onto a tin plate and he marvelled at the strength in her upper forearms—not fat and swaying like hammocks but hard, firm muscle—and the beads of sweat like an intricate tattoo on her forehead. He took the plate to the low wooden bench, sharing the space with two skinny men who looked as hungry as he was. No-one spoke, but he could feel all eyes on him as he tucked in. Like the food he had previously eaten, there was an absence of seasoning or spices, but this time there was a depth to the meat, a richness that was enough to satiate his desires.

'You like?' laughed the woman, and the younger girl rolled her eyes, and her large bee-stung lips clamped tight over a smile.

And Hugh understood now what was in the pot, and how the humour in the poster he could see hanging on the wall in the superintendent's office was misplaced. A cartoon chimp sitting in a cauldron with a red line across it. One of the many posters that Gerhard said were displayed across the village to stop the locals from eating the endangered animals. Put a missionary in the pot and it would have the same comic effect.

\* \* \*

'Wait,' Kate said incredulously. 'You ate a chimp?'

Hugh could tell that Kate was enjoying this. They hadn't spoken for a couple of days and she looked more relaxed than usual. He could see an empty wineglass at the corner of the screen.

'What did it taste like?'

'Like chicken.'

She laughed. 'We can't tell the kids—they'll be mortified!' He knew what she meant. They had stopped telling them they were eating roast lamb, instead calling it roast meat ever since little Maddie had made the connection.

'Tell me something else.'

'It rains all the time—because of the mountain.'

'Is it hot?'

'Not as hot as home.' Hugh could see she was wearing her singlet top and pyjama shorts, whereas he had a light windcheater on. 'What have you been up to?'

'The usual. The kids mostly. Oh, and Denise caught me running in bare feet to put the bin out again.'

It was an ongoing joke. How the old lady across the road had nothing else to do but watch her neighbours' every move and chastise Kate and the other younger women in the street for not wearing shoes on the blistering bitumen. Denise was English and had moved to the mining town in the seventies, and even after her husband had died and her children had left for Perth, she had stayed on in the small bungalow. A huge woman, who wore tent-like floral dresses, and as Kate had once remarked, had *grown to the size of her pond—like a koi*. It seemed as if all the women in the town had gotten larger over the years, those that stayed on in this small-pond life, and even Kate was a little fleshier these days, though Hugh didn't mind. There was more of her to cling on to at night.

'So, you're home at the end of the month?'

'I think it will blow out longer.'

'Wait—what?' He could see Kate leaning forward across the table and frowning so that a deep cleft formed between her brows.

'It will be longer.'

'How much longer? What about the holidays?'

'We weren't going anywhere.'

'The kids have VacSwim.'

He had forgotten the swimming lessons; his treasured role in spurring on his second child, Lucy, who was their bookworm and struggled with anything physical. He would miss the mornings at the town pool, the Indigenous children ducking and diving in the deep end whilst the white kids did their lessons back and forth in the designated lanes. Parents bonding over missed levels and lack of good tuition for the children.

'I'll email you the dates,' he answered, then to wind things up because he knew there was no point continuing with that frown, casually said, 'Love ya.'

Hugh waited for the reply, but Kate sat squinting at the screen, and then she disappeared, became a ghostly silhouette icon again.

Hugh glanced at the travel clock on his bedside table. It was late, but not late enough to attempt sleep, so he considered the book he had picked up in the mess. It was a Wilbur Smith novel, huge glossy lettering and a lion leaping across the front cover. He had a feeling he had read it years ago, with a different, more muted cover. He propped himself up with a pillow and spread his legs out on the bed. It was hard to concentrate on the printed words. He could hear sounds coming through the thin walls: a toilet flushing, then a gurgling and stammering of water through pipes. And then another sound, like a crying child. No, not a child, but Matt, sobbing on the other side of the wall. Hugh sat upright, not knowing whether he should cough and make a noise so that the young man would know he could be heard. Or did he really care? Most nights Hugh would half-catch the rambling phone calls to the girlfriend, sometimes angry rants that ended in love-worn murmurings as soft as a cocoon. And although Hugh only heard one side of the conversation, the man's point of view, it was clear that the girl was sleeping with other men and partying hard. In that first trip driving out to the mountain Matt had handed Hugh his phone, presenting it like a trophy, and there were the photos of Renee, all boobs and spidery eyelash extensions and a tan from a can, and he could see from her sculptured profile and jutty jaw that she was too much for soft-natured Matt.

The sobs were messy, embarrassingly so, and Hugh got up and walked with heavy steps to the cupboard. He opened the doors and banged them shut. Opened and closed the chest of drawers, but the sobs continued and Hugh wondered whether his generation were weaker than Carston's, and not made of the stern stuff that enabled them to leave their women behind in search of the iron roots of a mountain. He faked a cough, cleared his voice as if readying himself for a speech, and then the sobs became more muffled and gradually faded away so that all Hugh could hear was his own rapid breathing.

\*\*\*

Hugh woke at 5am, before his alarm went off, feeling as if he hadn't been asleep at all, or if he had, they were brief, unsatisfactory snatches where he dreamed mainly of the children, their laughs and screams distant cries like circling seabirds. There was a kink in the flimsy louvre blinds, and he could see the gradual glow of day creep through the gap. Soon it would take over the whole sky in that way you never see happening, when you can't know its true beginning. And then at dusk, the day would disappear in a different way, a sinking orange ball so easy to track before it dissolved to a stain on the horizon. And in all these different versions of light, the mountain range would always be a looming presence—sometimes a hazy, smoky outline, and sometimes that undeniable, unshakeable jaw.

Hugh was keen to get up. Today he would be journeying to the east side of the ranges to check out the chimpanzee colony with the environmental team, and he felt the relief of getting away from the campsite to see the mountain close up and drink in the colours and smells of the earth. Hugh had more samples, too, he wanted to collect, with always an eye out for rocks to bring home for the kids—ideally quartz or granite, so that they could be shattered for weeks in the rock tumbler, worn down into the best versions of themselves: smooth and soothing indents, to be stroked like worry stones. And, of course, high-grade powdery haematite for the girls, so sparkly that it looked as if it had been drenched in silver glitter.

* * *

Hugh dressed and made his way to the mess. It was too early for breakfast but he could get the first coffee from the urn, and catch up on emails before the day officially began. He was surprised to see others already up and about: a few African men who looked like village elders though dressed as pastors hurrying across the compound, one with a white shirt still with the telltale creases from its packet, those envelope-perfect folds. And Gerhard and the Chinese manager, Xiu, deep in conversation as they entered the mess hall before him. Hugh followed and stopped in surprise. There was the whole team, already gathered for breakfast, though now he could see no-one had drinks or food trays, and all eyes were on Gerhard and Xiu.

Hugh looked around and saw Matt standing with the other Australians. He walked across to stand next to him, but the younger man seemed embarrassed and looked down at the ground. Matt looked terrible: his face was deathly pale, though tiny pinpricks of colour dotted his neck like a colony of ants.

'What's going on?' Hugh asked him.

'Didn't you hear last night? One of the cooks has Ebola.'

Hugh turned to see that the kitchen was empty; a sterile,

eerie quietness filled the space. The women who were usually lugging pots and banging utensils were all gone. How did he not know about this? And it dawned on Hugh that the conversations he missed last night and every night, the half-delivered punchlines and the snatches he heard through the walls and cracks in doors, through playground quadrangles and high school corridors, were never meant for him but always floating out of reach, into unfathomable blue sky.

He didn't need to look at Gerhard and Xiu, could follow the essence of what was being said by watching the other men's expressions: the grim stare for *immediate lockdown*, the flatlined mouth for *twenty-one-day incubation period*, and the twitch of disdain on their lips for the woman who dared to cross over the Sierra Leone border and clutch the body of a dead relative days before the funeral. In their eyes he could see the deep-rooted disgust for leaking bodily fluids, for beads of sweat that could so easily fall into a pot of bubbling stew. Hugh felt his heart lurch. There were moments of life that cannot be reckoned with. Dead bodies to be washed and wept over; carrying the mummified remains of your children on your back until they wither away into a relic keepsake.

When Gerhard finished speaking, those with questions stepped forward—though not angry, or accusatory; just decent, ordinary men wanting answers, a voice of reason to assuage their fears. And Hugh knew enough about Gerhard to see that he was doing his best to be that person, but Hugh wanted more than that, craved a certain levity of feeling, the release valve of laughter that keeps you from falling deeper into yourself.

So, when the group of Australian men made their way out of the mess towards the accommodation block, Hugh moved along with them, to one of the cramped rooms, where the men leaned back, shoulder to shoulder, to share their stories about all those West African outrages.

Hugh felt a warmth swim over him and his throat began to soften, and he started telling the story about how Carston, in the seventies, had followed an uncharted river system down to the African coast, doing some prospecting along the way. Three days estimated travel time turned into a week, yet still they hadn't reached the coast and their supplies were dwindling dangerously. Suddenly they stumbled out of the jungle onto a beach, terrifying the locals who had never seen anyone come out of their jungle before. Carston showed them his iron ore samples, and his translator asked, *Have you seen anything like this before?* And the village men trembled. *Yes—yes. When it came, bad things happened. Chickens go missing—all our young men vanish.* Carston had asked to see what they meant but the villagers refused, the fear transforming their faces, until finally the translator persuaded them to change their minds. The tribal leader pointed to a special hut housing a shrine in the middle of the village, a shrine built to appease the new angry god. Carston went to look inside, and, lo, there was a stone tablet on which sat half a slaver's iron manacle.

There was a floating silence after Hugh finished talking. He could see that the story hadn't helped—it needed Carston for that—and there was a stricken look on Matt's face that might as well be saying, Are you telling us there is no God—no-one to call on, by whom we can be saved?

One man muttered, 'Fuck Ebola. This place has already given me the shits.' The men broke out in laughter, and that was Hugh's cue to quietly slip away.

He walked in the other direction, away from the accommodation block, his eyes on the distant villages and the tiny plumes of smoke puffing up like geysers all over the vast plains. There was the sound of gunfire going off, little spurts of anger shooting over the hazy-blue ranges, and Hugh wondered if the men were firing at each other or at strange, black-limbed creatures that hunched and crept through the forest.

He passed the security boom gate and could see that there was only one guard on duty now. The rest must have left last night to join the other fleeing staff. Behind the company-issued wraparound glasses, it was hard to tell what the man was thinking. Too difficult to tell if he was fearful or merely disinterested; whether he was stopping others from getting in, or stopping them from getting out. The guard shouted something, but Hugh just waved and kept on walking out of the campsite and along the dirt road towards the mountain. He had promised the kids he would bring back some rocks and he couldn't break his word now. And even if Kate would eventually throw them away, like his mother used to in her regular cleaning frenzies, his children would get to hold them at least once, feel the surety of the stone and imagine the warmth from whence they came.

# SEA WRACK

It was the idea of Venice that had made her want to buy into the canal development in the first place. A romanticised vision of water lapping against centuries-old stone, and watching the last light of the day soften like treacle around the boats' reflections. Of course, she had never been to Venice, nor smelled the perpetual stink said to rise from the trapped brown waters, especially in summertime. She had bought 19 Marine Terrace after only twenty searches on the Internet, one quick visit from Perth during her rostered day off and the slick spiel from the real estate agent, who told her there were three other buyers waiting with offers in the shadows.

*Don't be sucked into a Dutch auction*, warned her father, but she ignored him because she couldn't get past the word *Dutch* and likened it to the same provincial way he spoke about *Indian givers* and how *all Arabs are as mad as cut snakes*.

So for the past eighteen months she had lived with this flimsy, lightweight decision of hers, come to regret the unchanging view outside her window: the same two yachts permanently moored to adjacent pens, the undeveloped water frontages dotted with For Sale signs and scraggly ribbons of pigface. And stepping outside onto the decking—really her own private jetty with enough room for a French farmhouse table, a couple of deckchairs, and a pot of herbs—she also had to learn to live with the smell. A putrid, unrelenting stench, like a sucker punch to her nostrils. The first time she smelled it, she thought it was the briny water caught at low tide and brewed by the summer sun, or the gobs of fish bait that had congealed and hardened onto the wooden slats from where the young boys had been dipping fishing lines into the waters. But she eventually worked it out, stumbled across the source one hazy afternoon after a day of unpacking boxes and trying to reassemble IKEA bookshelves without the original manuals. She needed to get some fresh air, so headed out to finally explore the beach south of the marina, and as she neared the dunes and the vivid blue waters cast as an eye into the curve of the coast, the smell became unmistakably sulphurous. Like rotten eggs. And then as she cleared the top of the dunes she saw it, the wall of seaweed, which was so shocking, so unexpected it could have been a mound of corpses left to rot and dry out in the sand. Far along the coast she could see it, this spanning wall of weed, and in the shallows more of it lapping and eddying closer and closer to shore.

'It's a sight, isn't it?'

She hadn't noticed the man taking photographs, a scarf fashioned as a mask over his nose and mouth.

'It looks terrible.'

'That's the least of our problems,' he said.

'What do you mean?'

'Toxic fumes. Cancer clusters.'

'Sorry?'

'You're not from around here, are you?'

'No. I just arrived.'

'Didn't you hear about this?'

'Not in the city.'

'I'd go back.'

'I can't. I just bought a townhouse on the marina.'

His eyes said it all. They widened, and with a slight flicker reflected back a version of herself as a fool.

His name was Phillip Jordan. She was to find out later that he was responsible for the Port Action Group blog and the photos that were posted weekly of the seaweed mountain from different angles. Sometimes there were artistic close-ups of the fresh weed, fringed, translucent amber, with delicate popping balls, and other times huge jarring photos emblazoned with the words 'Save Our Beach'.

She tried to work it all out at the first meeting she attended, listening to the residents talk about how the canals were poorly designed and engineered so that the sea wrack had become trapped and unable to wash naturally back to sea and why they couldn't sue the developer—the company had since gone broke. And not just an environmental disaster—the dugongs robbed of a natural food source—but there were the illnesses: the unexplained headaches and rashes, the sudden loss of weight, and the lethargy, where your body could barely move from the couch and your head felt like the greatest weight in the world. And as she listened to the voices, which ached with pent-up hysteria, she studied Phillip and the young girl of maybe ten or eleven sitting next to him, a blonde-thatched stick insect, covered in scales of eczema, a dried-out wisp of a girl. And the way he bent his head close to her ear, patiently explaining things, and his patterned scarf, a loose bib around his neck, and those faded, torn pair of Levi's—all these things told her that he was the kind of husband who would have used the expression 'We're pregnant!' when telling friends of their baby-to-be.

He caught her staring, and gave a half-committed smile in her direction, maybe recognising her from the beach, though she wasn't sure. She tried to focus on the speaker, a thin retiree with a broken-down voice, but she couldn't get past the words she had seen on Phillip's blog. *Sea wrack*. At first she was surprised that she didn't know this term (and her being the wordsmith!), but now it bothered her because it wasn't neutral sounding like seaweed, or sargassum (a soothing salve in the mouth), but biting and shrewish on her tongue. *Sea wrack. Shipwreck. Homewrecker. Racked with guilt...*

Two more meetings went on like this until she realised that by living directly on the canals she was considered the enemy, and there was no way back from that.

\*\*\*

The water shot a rippled light across the computer screen, forcing her to move further into the living room and away from the sun streaming through the glass doors. The brightness made it hard to concentrate, and she faltered on the next word. The deadline for the report was almost upon her but she had barely started. She could only imagine what Ann Marie would say about that. Six months ago they were in the sprawling departmental office, desks suggesting separation—this is my area of expertise, this is yours—and Ann Marie swivelling her chair across from the other side and saying, *Greg must be bonkers to let you do this.*

Bonkers, or feeling sorry for the woman who was clearly unravelling before his eyes. Yes, definitely crazy—for he should have known that she would be unreliable, break the promise that she could do the same job working remotely, producing the same quality output and submitting her work on time. He must have known that her mental state was fragile at the best of times.

She didn't want to think about Greg, pushed those uneasy feelings aside and tried to focus on the work at hand. She typed: 'Western Australian regional unemployment rates', and then stopped. It was no use. She got up, put the kettle on and waited, staring out the window. In this harsh light she could see that the decking, bleached and grainy grey, needed resealing, and there were nails that were working their way out of the wood like foreign bodies being dispelled from the skin. Another item to add to the list of things to do—or not to do, as she suspected would be the case. Her father had been right all along about the house. The impracticality of the painted weatherboarding that would need to be redone in a few years' time—this row of quaint, pastel-coloured terrace houses turning into a blistering, flaky eyesore under the full brunt of the sun. And her father more distressed for the work that he felt obliged to help her with, especially now that she was on her own and so was he.

Suddenly her eyes alighted on a movement through the water—a rare thing here, apart from circling seagulls or a white flip of fish belly—and she could make out a yacht creeping past the heads into the marina. She went out through the doors and onto the deck, tracking its passage through the labyrinthine waterways, wondering if anyone else was witnessing this small miracle—doubtful with most of the buildings empty, the wealthy owners able to afford to walk away from their failed holiday investment. She wanted to share this with someone, test out her voice, as she hadn't spoken in days, but there was no-one around. So she found herself waving to the lone yacht, taking on the role of a harbour master welcoming the sailor home to the shore. To her surprise, the yacht slowly made its way to her, and she could see there was a solitary figure on board waving back.

'Is it okay to moor here?' he shouted.

She stared at the man, still surprised at how the boat had made it this far.

'Yes... It's my pen. It came with the house.'

'Thanks.'

He brought the boat closer and then threw a large rope to her. She stood there dumbly, watching whilst he jumped off the boat and secured the thick rope to the pylon.

'Rob.' He held out his hand and she gave it a quick squeeze. He was taller than she had expected and the extra height made her catch her breath.

'I'm Katrina. I'm surprised you got through.'

She could see the dark weed caught around the hull and trailing like bony fingers into the water.

'Yeah—I didn't realise until too late. Where's the marina office?'

'Oh, it's unmanned. I mean, the whole place has shut down.'

'There must be someone around.'

'I don't know much about these things.'

And it was true, she didn't know anything. Had no idea about the ins and outs of sailing, the difference between a skiff and a ketch, a bow and a stern. No interest whatsoever in boats and ocean faring, though she loved the fact that other people did, took the risks on her behalf whilst she sat sipping chardonnay on the shore.

'I might take a look around—see if I can talk to someone who knows.'

She nodded, wishing to be of more use, as she watched the lanky man walk away to where the jetty met up with the main boardwalk. She should have kept him there with questions. Asked about his American accent, why he was so far from home—though judging by his tanned limbs, flowing hair and beard flecked a salty grey she suspected that he had lost the concept of a home long ago. And the name of the yacht, *Endymion*? Now there was an entry point for conversation, an opportunity to discuss Keats and her love of poetry, and how her father had convinced her to switch from a Major in English Literature to Economics because there was no money in writing, and how instead she had fallen into writing policy for the State Government on the area of employment and the labour market, and now her heart wasn't in it any more. Rob was gone before she could speak about any of that, and as she walked back inside to resume her work—the smell of rotten egg wafting from the dunes—she felt a slight throb in her temples.

She didn't have to wait long to have her questions answered. A few hours later Rob appeared at the glass doors, and after letting this stranger in, she soon discovered he was originally from the Napa Valley, had worked in a start-up company in San Francisco in the nineties making a tidy fortune and then, for want of a better word, a mid-life crisis took him on a decade-long sailing odyssey, where he got to sleep every night beneath the moon's mellow glow. That was the source of the yacht's name: Endymion, the ancient Greek myth about the beautiful sleeping man watched and adored by the moon goddess, Selene. Rob had never heard of Keats and a quizzical smile formed on his lips as she recited the opening stanza.

She offered him a glass of local wine (almost as good as from the Napa!) and he wandered around her living room as if looking for clues: the stack of *Gourmet Traveller* magazines on the coffee table, the ornate 1920s mirror over the mantelpiece, the collection of photos of nieces and friends' children. But it was the framed orange-and-gold threaded kimono that interested him the most.

'Have you been to Japan?'

'No, a friend was an exchange student. I love the fabric so much—it's like a work of art.'

'It's a pity to frame it. You should wear it.'

She didn't know what to say to that. Found herself talking at super-speed about the need to preserve the heritage of the kimono as the garments were being hacked to pieces and the fabric sold off to make mobile phone and iPod covers for tourists. She wasn't sure why she was rushing. Maybe it was this feeling that time was running out, and like a speed date, any minute now he would hear a better story from the next candidate. He watched her, still with that smile playing at his lips, and she couldn't work out if he liked her or thought she was ridiculous. It was only when he suggested they take the next bottle of wine to his yacht that she thought maybe he was interested after all.

The yacht seemed smaller once she was on it, and for a man who had wealth, rather dingy and worn. In the cabin area she had to double over to reach the table, and once she was sitting on the bench chair she could feel the uneven, ripped vinyl bite at her skin through her skirt. There was a bundle of dirty clothes rolled up in a corner, and the table was covered in crumbs and old coffee cup stains.

'So tell me about yourself.'

She winced a little at his words, but the wine softened any resistance, and she was surprised at how the words flowed and how much she was willing to reveal. She heard herself talking about her first marriage, to a fellow university student, the Guild President, who had hopes of a career in federal politics, but ended up working for the local branch of the maritime union instead. Those were the days when you could only access Victoria Quay with a security badge, and a steady flow of ships passed in and out to dock, some seasonal—the triple-banked row of Japanese tuna boats— and some seemingly permanent, such as the *Cormo Express*, a bankrupted livestock carrier with its rusted gangway teetering like a giant praying mantis's leg, where the fat-bottomed girls in black denim, the 'wharf rats', would sneak up and down, trading their bodies for cigarettes.

The marriage was never going to last. Too many late nights in the Fremantle pubs took its toll, and his boyish body thickened and turned slack. *Fat lush*, she had joked, but there was too much truth in what she said and they parted before the bitterness truly set in. What she didn't say was that years later she had bumped into him at a mutual friend's party, and there he was, looking toned and taut with a pretty new wife on his arm, and it occurred to her that she might have been the source of his unhappiness all along.

'I married Gilligan and ended up with the Skipper,' she said to Rob, and got the laugh she was aching for. 'So what about you? Any wives I should know about?'

'I don't stay in one place long enough.'

'Maybe that's why you're circumnavigating the world. Running away from any commitment.'

A shadow passed over his face. 'Why do women always say the same things?'

'Maybe you always end up with the same kind of woman.'

He couldn't help but smile, and they continued to talk, slowly getting drunker. Later, she was to blame the alcohol for why she broke her usual rule of never sleeping with someone on the first date. If only they had gone back to her house there wouldn't have been the incessant rocking of the waves to make her unsteady on her feet, causing her to stumble to her knees, nor the sickening smell of wrack to make her smother her face against his crotch; there wouldn't have been the thrusting of a penis, skinny like a pencil, out of sync with the rhythm of her hips. She left him snoring on his back and crept back to her jetty guided by the light of the moon. She showered straightaway, allowing the water to sluice away the taint of his unwashed body and the stickiness smeared across her thighs. *Semen, Seaman, See me*—normally she would have enjoyed this wordplay, but there was nothing to joke about now. She had basically slept with a hobo.

The next morning, she felt relief when she saw the yacht was no longer moored in front of her place. She could imagine the hull strangled by more weed as it exited the harbour, pulling a tangled brown mess in its wake. There was a pang of loss as she realised she had left her good pair of Milano glassware on board.

She had this sudden urge to ring Greg, but she knew he would be having his morning coffee with his wife before he left for work, his voice becoming strained and furtive as he fobbed her off on his mobile in that usual, detached managerial tone of his while she begged and pleaded with him not to end their affair. She had never thought about his children before, but now she could picture them sitting at the breakfast table, too: little blonde-haired stick insects, sweet and sickly and desperate for attention.

The headache, which had been there all along, was pounding fiercely at her skull, and a ruptured light like jagged starbursts rimmed her vision. Even though it was still very early, there was enough sunlight streaming through the glass to show up every speck of dust and dirt. She was shocked at how filthy this place had become and set about wiping down and then scrubbing every surface until her back and neck ached. She began to dust the framed kimono, then stopped to stare at the exquisite shimmering fabric, wondering how the embroidered silk would feel against her skin. It was tempting to remove the garment from its glass casing, but she knew the beauty would disappear all too quickly. The way it did when as a child she would run up to her father with a bucketful of shells, and see how disappointing and dull they became once removed from the sea.

# THREAD

It was wrong of them to come, but here they were, being greeted by the minister with his trailing white sleeves and mouth strained like a button through the hole in his dark, woolly beard. Above them, a sign quilted in bargain-bin remnants welcomed all to the True Life Anglican Church.

Katherine felt small and stooped in the bungalow-shaped building where the low white ceiling topped their heads like icing on a wedding cake. No, they shouldn't even be here, she thought, but it was too late to consider leaving now, with the minister looking so biblical in his robes and beard, and welcoming them so warmly. A fisherman's beard at that, she noted, and was at least heartened by this observation.

'Welcome. You've not been here before?'

'We usually go to the city service,' answered Katherine, aware that her voice sounded loud and shrill, when she had hoped it to be tempered with a sort of gentle regret. A voice that implied, We're sorry we can never be members of your church.

'Glad you came,' he answered, nodding his head, and Katherine immediately felt bad. After all, it was her husband's fault they were here, and this calm, good-natured man had to stand there and be civil to them. She sensed her husband standing just behind her, and was angry that he compelled her to speak, just as he made her deal with the hawkers at the front door and send his family their birthday cards every year. It was this reluctance, this holding just a little further back from where she was in life, that annoyed her.

Katherine spoke. 'We slept in, so we couldn't make it in time to get to the city. My husband forgot to set the alarm,' and then immediately wished she hadn't said a word, because she might as well have been saying, I blame my husband for everything in my life.

She wondered what on earth the minister would be thinking of her now, but his biblical blue eyes maintained a steady, unblinking gaze and she knew he was the sort of person to think the best of everyone.

'Let me introduce my wife, Shirley,' he answered, calling over a stout woman dressed in a red suit. Shirley gave Katherine a grim, cursory once-over and nodded.

'Welcome. Here are the chorus books and the programs. Sit anywhere you like, but keep the first two rows free.' She seemed to speak beyond Katherine, keeping her eyes focused on the swinging glass entry doors, in case there was someone else she should be talking to.

'Thank you,' replied Katherine, smiling at the minister, her voice invested with more than just gratitude. She sensed his trials were many with Shirley by his side.

Katherine and her husband walked over to the white plastic chairs, which were laid out like rows of teeth. Some families, already scattered around the hall, had pulled the chairs out of alignment; were leaning back, scraping, rocking and dragging the chairs away from the others in the row. Children with dampened hair and new shoes, not quite sitting or standing, strained to see their friends in the next aisle. It had the same sense of impermanence as a picnic.

Katherine chose to sit in the back row, and her husband followed her. Usually she liked walking down to the front of her church, past the aisles of gleaming pews and the straight-backed men in dark suits. The harpsichord would be sounding out a triumphant hymn and Katherine would almost march along like a homebound soldier down the aisle to the second row from the front. She liked this kind of ritual, she would always tell her husband, the music—the melodic line soaring with the spirit—the people all laid out like the alphabet, and the solidity of the wood beneath her legs as she slid her soft dress across the pew.

However, this Sunday she wanted to keep her distance and become more of a spectator in this sorry affair. The room was now three-quarters filled, she saw, and hummed with snatches of conversation. And the congregation looked surprisingly multicultural for this suburb. There were Asian families, Indian families and even African families. It's beginning to look like a UNICEF greeting card, she decided, half-wishing to tell her husband. But she could detect the faint sour smell of breakfast on his breath, and instead turned her head away. Just then, a reedy sound filled the room, and Katherine noticed a woman with a pince-nez perched on her thin nose playing the Lowrey organ set up in the corner. Katherine caught her breath as Shirley fired up the overhead projector and straightened the song lyric transparency, which was written in the kind of writing found on the nameplates in family bibles.

Oh, Lord! Choruses, not hymns, she thought, while the whole bedraggled congregation rose to their feet and sang in meek, half-formed voices. The minister, flowing in glorious robes, glided down the centre, followed by another robed minister, who was black-skinned and looked like he came from a distant continent. That must be his family over there, two rows in front of her—the wife, and the three small children. Yes, a missionary family visiting Australia for training, and it all was beginning to come together for her while she studied the backs of their heads and the napes of their necks. The woman's hair was plaited across her scalp, little perfect bumps and knobs that Katherine wished to read as if Braille. Her own mother wore her long, dark hair in thick plaits, and had gone to the hairdresser's the day she turned thirty to have them cut off in two consecutive snips, so that they fell, *thump thump*, to the ground like useless limbs. They were kept for years in white tissue paper, and colourless rubber bands clinched the fat braids together. They disgusted Katherine so much, these remnants of her mother's glossy girlhood, and yet she needed to hold the firm, woven strands in her fists as if they were unwieldy ropes of existence. Oh, the texture; the silk and tenacity of such things, and the colour as rich and tart as burnt raisins. But nothing compared to these African heads. The beautiful shape of the skull, really an elongated crown—why, she could almost think of a proud queen, or a ripening insect sac—whereas the others in the room, the thin perms, the bouffant bobs, had heads as round and as ordinary as a doodle on a notepad.

So Katherine studied scalps, overly laundered collars, moles, profiles, the way she could see through the piercings in earlobes, the lint on jackets, her own dry, small hands, and then homed in on the voice of the minister, as he spoke the words of the Apostle Paul: 'Wives submit yourselves unto your own husbands, as unto the Lord.' Katherine glanced around at the women's faces expecting reaction, yet no-one seemed to be concerned; if anything, the mothers looked rather bored and worn out.

The heat rose in Katherine's face. She watched the bearded man continue, saw how his African counterpart mimicked his posture and expression (so vacant and full of male piety), and how the minister's lips were thin and cruel through the beard, and the eyes that cool ice floe of people who watch but never see. And Shirley, poor fat Shirley, wearing the hot, itchy red suit for him, and having to make small chit-chat when she would rather be safe in a corner somewhere. What a dreadful church, she decided. Full of such awful people, the men (clearly misogynists), and such a low, flat roof that could never possibly house the presence of God.

Katherine wanted to leave but the only door had been shut, and the room somehow felt hermetically sealed. There were no windows (she had never noticed this before), and she longed for the jewelled panes of glass that seemed to break the darkness in her own church like glowing embers. Or even like panels of a vision. A vision fired up by the sun in a great expanse of darkness. Yes, yes, this is what she longed for more than anything.

Then Katherine noticed the spider. From a single, almost invisible thread, it descended from the ceiling as if it was a tiny abseiler. The movement was slow and deliberate, its fat, black body dropping like a lure into silent water. Katherine watched, fascinated. The spider's squat legs were crouched in a warrior stance while the two front legs moved furiously to weave the next strand of web. And it continued this descent, slowly, the front legs whirring and spinning, until there was no doubt in Katherine's mind that it would come to rest on the head of the woman sitting in the chair in front of her.

Katherine turned to tell her husband, but he was already watching. 'Shall we say something?' she whispered. He didn't answer, but squeezed her hand instead.

Together, they watched transfixed as the spider hovered above the shiny henna-coloured bob, and then disappeared into the hair in one final sickening lurch.

'We need to tell her,' she commanded her husband, but he gripped Katherine's hand even tighter.

Katherine felt ill. She looked around at the congregation, but all their heads were bowed in silent prayer. Rows and rows of obedient heads. And the spider's image wouldn't leave her alone. There was that fat, satisfied body; the fast and furious weaving; the steady drop, and then gone, as if it had drowned forever in the beautiful hair. Would there be others, she wondered, looking up and half expecting a regiment of spiders to be falling from the ceiling. She felt her husband's hand squeeze hers again and turned to look at him. He nodded towards the woman in front. The spider was retreating slowly from the hair, ascending on the same long, silvery thread.

Then her husband announced in a low, calm voice, 'It has attached a web to her scalp.'

And sure enough, she saw he was right. The woman moved her head slightly, and the thread swayed at the same moment, still intact, like a celestial cord. A single thread, and suddenly everything was made so clear. Yes, Katherine understood now. The underslung bungalow, the bearded minister, the African novice, those rows and rows of bending, prayerful, obedient heads, and she knew she would go home and discuss the meaning of it all, until the words became like paper on her tongue, and her husband would say, 'Enough, Katherine. Enough.'

# LAST DAYS IN DARWIN

*Joy Luck Club*

My mother isn't Chinese. Nor are her friends—'the girls', they call themselves, at fifty-three years of age. But every Tuesday afternoon they play mah-jong. They unfold the cider-coloured card table and set up the plastic tiles. Dainty crustless sandwiches are passed around on the lacquered Chinese bamboo tray. Sweet sherry is poured by the thimbleful.

There is quiet Mavis, dressed in the pattern of yesteryear. Her simple outline has been sheared from generic floral cottons and stitched at home with the whirring black Singer. *A little lady*, the others often remark to their daughters on those mother–daughter occasions.

Mavis bakes banana cakes. Moist, golden slabs that are generously sliced and smell of sweet bread straight from the oven. The cake falls apart on the fork, rippling with the treacled banana and the fine black lace. When she laughs, it is done neatly, through small, childish teeth. Her hands, burdened with old family rings, fall into claps on her lap. Concern fixes itself on her brow in lines of varying length, like children's counting rods. Before she goes home, she always leaves a little something in the freezer for Don, my dad.

Quite different from Kay, who is bossy but kind. Kay thrives on housework and charity drives. She swaps cleaning stories as people swap tales of love, but her war against dirt is always the most passionate. The others are in awe, and always make sure they wipe the top of the fridge before she calls in; she is very tall and could easily get to those out-of-reach places without the aid of a kitchen stool. At school she played hockey, and she still keeps that same fearless stride through life, pushing through shops and doctors' surgeries as if she was three steps behind a little white ball. By the end of the day her large bones ache, and the knots on her calves swell to purple and blue. But she never complains, just avoids Bermuda shorts and going dancing late at night. Kay applies lipstick by memory. Smears the bright coral across her lips in a brusque, mannish swipe. She always supplies Mavis with a Coles bag warm with the deliquescence of banana.

Dianne is the groomed one of the group. She plays tennis in girlish pleats. Her hair is a frosted bouffant which over the years has diminished in height. One day she will resort to wearing a wig. Her head is generous. Large and bony, it is a canvas for all of her emotions, while her body, frail from the years of dieting, maintains an elegant reserve. She speaks of other people's husbands in order to bring up her own, who is successful and very wealthy. Dianne has a joie de vivre that is infectious. She uses the word 'fun' as people once used the word 'gay'.

My mother. Surrounded by her girlfriends, laughing and playing mah-jong. She isn't Chinese. Though today she looks tired and her skin is stretched like Chinese nankeen, tightly, from cheekbone to cheekbone. There is something Asiatic or maybe Indian in her look. An ancient glimpse of bone and wisdom pressing through the buff-toned skin.

## *Fortunes*

My sister is complaining again about the vegetables. 'These are more expensive than in London. They call this a lettuce?'

We are both in a bad mood. The Parap shop is a convenient minimart, only a five-minute walk from our parents' house. We took the car. As Yvonne discovered, linen suits, like salad vegetables, lose their life-force in the Darwin humidity. To sweat and breathe in stifling air, a filmy perfumed strangeness—all this is okay in another country. However, when everyone is wearing KingGee shorts and thongs, and buying white sliced bread, it is simply all too much.

'I'm sick of hicksville,' Yvonne hisses.

We've left Mum with the mah-jong group. For a woman who is supposed to be dying, she still arranges those tiles with the precision of a winner. She is dying. Yvonne left her life behind because she is dying and now here Mum is, gossiping and scuttling tiles across a table.

'Shall we get some scratchies?' I ask.

For some reason this abbreviation doesn't irritate my sister as much as 'undies' or 'boosies'.

'Yes. Let's get four more.'

All month we have been buying these instant lottery tickets and taking them home to Mum. A tradition has been established. I laughingly blow kisses on them and sing out, *Come on Lady Luck*. Sometimes Mum is too tired to sit up, so she lets us scratch out the games on her behalf. No-one really cares about the money. It's merely an attempt to revise a future that doesn't exist. Perhaps to tempt fate with possibility.

Driving around Darwin streets, running errands for Mum, opposing traffic—both of us scream out the car window, *We beat Darwin!* If only Mum would do the same.

## *Fractions*

My mother is a quarter Greek. It's not very fashionable to be Greek in Darwin. People still talk about the cyclone, and how the Greek men dressed in drag so they could be airlifted out with the women and children. I wasn't born until a year later and it's difficult to imagine Uncle Vic in a seersucker frock. Mum only admits to her origins whenever people mention Paspaley pearls.

My sister and I are an eighth Greek. In this light, with the sun filtering through the green fibreglass shading, Yvonne looks almost tubercular, and her pale hair, pulled back tight in a bun and straining against the roots, absorbs the colour like a thirsty plant. I notice for the first time how my sister has aged. The face powder crumbles a little on her skin, gathers in the crease around the nose and in the sad, fine lines near her mouth. A poor mask, loosening its hold on her face. And around her ears where the hair strains hardest, the tender pink places of childhood.

I have a nose that would look good profiled on a silver coin. My grandfather had a censorious mouth. Nana still lives in the same old house by the beach. A Queenslander—all stilts and weatherboard timber. She is famous for her wishbones. Across a line of grocer's string attached to her kitchen curtain rod, she has hung the crooked bones to dry. They divine the ceiling. Mangy and yellow, the ones with meat still attached glisten like glue.

'Make a wish,' she says, and before I can prise the magic bone apart, it snaps like a twig in the crook of my little finger.

'That chicken has osteoporosis,' she laughs, but her eyes always betray the sadness.

## *Petulance*

My mother has a refractory jaw. She has been chewing on that bean patty for ages. She chews everything into one stubborn fibrous wad, like a giant hairball to be coughed out later.

'Everything is tasteless,' she says like a naughty child. Her jawbone, large and defiant, is an unhinged relic.

Today, Mum insists on going to the Mindil Beach Markets. We arrange her body in the wheelchair in a way that will reduce the weight on her bones. Any pressure can cause untold grief. So there she is, a rag-doll mother folded into a respectable mother shape, and we set off for the outing.

When we arrive at the markets, we wheel Mum across some sand and stop behind the fruit salad stall. But the smell of Asian cookery is startling. Hot drifts of oil-saturated noodles, char kway teow, pork dumplings, spicy laksa, beaded sticks of dry satay—all assault the sea air. Now we realise why she has insisted on coming.

Initially I refuse to buy the kway teow. 'It will ruin your cancer diet,' I protest.

But both Dad and Yvonne turn on me angrily. 'Lighten up, Sylvia.'

Tears prick the underside of my eyelids. I can feel my red-gilled lids burn. I walk through the crowds of tourists and locals blanketed in these red-hot lids. I don't expect to see anyone I know. Most kids don't stick around once they've left school. Because I don't expect to see anyone, I assume no-one can see me. My eyelids are a blood-lined hood.

The man serving the food has a broad, flat nose and full lips. His black eyes are shallow in the orbits. Blackheads scatter his nose like apple seeds within a pale core.

He transfers a tongful of slippery noodles into a plastic container and squeezes a lid on tight. It squelches. Through the plastic, I can feel the grease slide.

I return to Mum and give her the food. She eats it, crying out with every mouthful: 'I can taste it. At long last I can taste food.'

We wheel her around the stalls. There are the usual racks of faded tie-dyed clothing and batik skirts and trousers. Trestle tables are covered in wooden carvings that seem pointless once taken from the holiday country. An artist sketches a woman. His approach is close to that of a political caricaturist. He dramatically alters the proportions of her face. She is given silly eyebrows and an Afghan nose. A man in the small crowd—possibly her husband—shrinks back uncomfortably, and flicks through second-hand books at a nearby stall. Maybe he has seen a version of his wife he doesn't know.

I walk away and stand by a white elephant stall. A belt buckle catches my eye. It is a round, glassy mound in which a little sea horse has been preserved. The sea horse is orange and dragon-like. Its body is covered in a delicate scaled armoury. The body and tail curve back in a sweet embryonic curl. The effect is so ethereal that I feel like shaking the sphere to see if a light blanket of snow falls.

'Dr Grey! Dr Grey!'

My mother is making a scene. It's her doctor she's calling to, and he can't seem to hide his embarrassment. One of his patients—close to death—sits in a wheelchair at a popular family market and calls out his name. He wavers for a moment, then leaves his family and comes over.

'Mrs Maine. How are we today?' He adopts the same manner as in the surgery but it doesn't look right in those leisurewear slacks. The ones the colour of shark fin.

'I'm fighting fit,' she answers, just like a good girl. 'I even have my appetite back. I just ate an enormous lunch.' Her smile is skeletal and glassy. An intimation of the corpse-to-be. The doctor smiles dumbly in return.

'Is that your family over there?' Mum points to the two small boys standing nearby, watching them. The doctor is hesitant. He knows damn well who she is pointing at, but squints his eyes as if to make out their outlines.

'Ah… The boys. Yes.' Before Mum has a chance to call them over, he pats her hands briskly. 'I must be off now.'

He leaves so quickly—pulls the small boys along, kite-tail trailing, so fast—that he doesn't hear or smell the retching stench of vomit. There on the white sand lies a pile of char kway teow that looks remarkably like the original meal.

## *Theorem*

The minister arrives. I dislike him immediately. He is smarmy and religious. Tall. He stoops his head over like a biblical crook, not knowing what to do with the extra top inches. An affected humility. He is probably the first generation of his family to have such height.

He wears thick metal-framed glasses, and the watery green of his eyes swells in the distortion.

My sister has warned me already about ministers. Something about slurping their tea and hairy ears. Yvonne has many theories. *Never see a local band with a name ending in a 'z' instead of an 's'. Only members of the Royal Family can wear white shoes. Cats and spurned lovers can look after themselves.*

Surely five minutes in the company of a minister with cake crumbs adhered to his chin is no worse than ten minutes listening to Boyz Night Out at the local tavern? For a man of the cloth, he certainly is in need of a napkin. I pour him another cup of tea. I notice that where the sock's elastic ripples his leg, the skin is cadaverous.

Mum is arranging her own funeral. She is famous for being sensible. She has chosen 'Morning Has Broken' and 'Amazing Grace' as her hymns. She loves to sing but I guess in this case it really doesn't matter. Today she looks tired, and arranges her arms and legs on the sofa as if they are pieces of kindling. Death slowly bruises the area beneath her eyes.

Yvonne thinks funerals are just like weddings. Another theory involving rites of passage or something. The last wedding was for Maisie's eldest, my cousin Peter. That day there were lots of hymns, and white doilies pressed around slabs of loam-coloured fruit cake. I wore a long black crimplene dress and painted my face white. Only my eyebrows had stood out, drawn as crazy bolts of lightning. Mum was furious with me. I didn't care. I had matters of identity to sort out. I was yet to learn that being Gothic didn't work in bright, clean, sunny Darwin. And I never knew that a cancer inched along my mother's spine like a live, singing wire.

The minister gets up to leave, and for one brief moment my mother looks frightened.

'Can we say a prayer?' she says quietly.

He looks surprised. He adjusts his glasses and prisms of rainbow light stream through the room. I have this feeling that beneath the magnified glass, his eyes are straining hard into a tiny mole crumple. He doesn't see my mother at all.

## *Colours*

My mother is dying. She lies on the bed she has shared with Dad for thirty years. Death isn't black, I seem to notice. It's a mulberry blue. I show Mum's feet to Yvonne. I think I'm trying to shock her or something. Maybe to prove to her that Mum is dying after all. Her feet are blue. Together we watch the ghostly stains appear on the entire body. Veins collapsing and the body flooded with the cool wash of indigo. Return to earth.

Earlier we had tried to lift Mum onto the commode. Her thin nightie stuck like a second skin to her small frame. Yvonne tried to peel the fabric from beneath Mum's wishbone pelvis so she could pee into the ceramic bowl. A few drops of pale yellow issued. I handed Yvonne the toilet paper and she wiped underneath, the mysterious cleft a dark wink of folded skin. We laid Mum back on the bed, the nightie pulled down to restore her modesty. I stroked her head and felt the solid strength contained within the skull. Her mind's ark. The rest of her was disappearing fast, but the head's dimensions were secured in bone. What was left of her hair was plastered over the skull, like a child still moist from the afterbirth.

And every ten minutes she changes colour. A multi-speckled, bruised canvas. She is a giant lily one moment, large arterial branches running across the silent pad, life's ink moving slowly along the plant-like pathways. Next, a yellow stone on a riverbed. Death closes her petal by petal. She begins to shrink back, small, within her paper skin.

## *Endings*

Mum is now a piece of driftwood. I'm scared to touch her in case she breaks into pieces and slips through my hands. Yvonne is organising the clothes to give to the undertaker. She chooses the dress that Mum wore to Peter's wedding. A lovely soft, pleated silk. There is a matching handbag, but the shoes no longer fit. Mum's feet are swollen like fat tribal canoes.

I become frantic. 'Mum can't go barefoot,' I yell at my sister.

Yvonne calms me down. She finds some beige nylon stockings to cover Mum's legs and two artificial daisies to thread between the fat toes. Mum is to be the Princess Bride. A dancer with red shoes that finally split and burst open like ripened fruits. Figs—not mangoes, though. The smell of rotting mango is too familiar now, too cloying.

Downstairs I can hear Nana doing the dishes. Her sleeves are rolled back to reveal her strong, bare arms. I can hear the *dip dip* of dish into water and suds, and the final sluice as she rinses things clean. I imagine her lifting her arms, and the cotton sleeves rustling. The smell of lavender briefly escapes from her skin. A lightly dusted, female sadness. Always, the smell of grandmothers.

## ACKNOWLEDGEMENTS

These stories would not exist without the love, patience and support of so many friends, family and colleagues. So a big shout-out to my beautiful writing goddesses: Maureen Gibbons, Maria Papas and Dee Pfaff—your wisdom and gift of words have helped shape and refine these stories. Thank you to my very first beta reader, Rebecca Braasch, for her friendship and laughter; Jodie How, for the insightful writerly advice; and the Dampier, Rossy and Rivo friends for your sustaining encouragement. To Caroline and John Wood, heartfelt gratitude for supporting the local writing scene and giving me (and others) a much-needed break with the Margaret River Short Story Competition. Thank you to the incredible talents of the editorial team of Josephine Taylor and Camha Pham, it was a joy working with you both. Thank you to Debra Billson for the fabulous cover. I am also indebted to the generosity of established writers such as Laurie Steed, Evan Fallenberg, Laura Elvery and Cate

ACKNOWLEDGEMENTS

Kennedy who helped pave the way. Some of these stories were previously published, so thank you to the following publications and their editorial teams: 'The Egg', *Kill Your Darlings*, October edition, 2018; 'Warm Bodies', *Westerly Magazine*, *Flux*, October 2017; 'The Shape of Things', *Review of Australian Fiction*, vol. 13, issue 1, 2015; 'In Transit', *SALA Anthology*, Arts Council of Mansfield, 2015; 'Dying', *The Trouble with Flying and Other Stories*, Margaret River Press, 2014; 'The Bees of Paris', *Knitting and Other Stories*, Margaret River Press, 2013; 'Last Days in Darwin', *HQ Magazine*, November issue, 1996.

Finally, thank you to my family, The Pritchards, Nairns, Millers and Fites, especially Dad and Ann who came to every reading, no matter how small, Susan Cole for sharing her life and being an inspiration in many ways, my brother Kim (the funniest guy I know), and my late mother, Sandy, who used to lovingly type up my first attempts at poetry. Love and thanks to my darling twin sister, Karyl, who is always my greatest cheerleader from the front stalls of London, and of course Stuart, Freya and Martha (my teenage adviser!) who help anchor me to the best part of my life.